Big changes are going on all around Jessie.

Jessie's just entered a performing arts school where she can work on her goal of becoming a great actress. It's fun and exciting but also hard, much harder than Jessie could have ever imagined it to be. The stacks of homework are one thing, and all the new faces are more than enough to try to remember. Jessie wants to fit in, but she's worried—about her grades, about what her classmates think of her, and about the boy who likes her. Most of all, Jessie worries about herself and something she can't change—her dark brown skin. She's been hiding a secret that makes her feel ugly and unloved, especially compared to her golden-skinned sister. It's hurting her work and her friendships. When you're hiding something so big, it's hard to be honest with anyone. Will Jessie ever be able to open up?

Fiction

Fall Secrets

CANDY DAWSON BOYD

PUFFIN BOOKS

PUFFIN BOOKS
Published by the Penguin Group
Penguin Books USA Inc., 375 Hudson Street, New York, New York 10014, U.S.A.
Penguin Books Ltd, 27 Wrights Lane, London W8 5TZ, England
Penguin Books Australia Ltd, Ringwood, Victoria, Australia
Penguin Books Canada Ltd, 10 Alcorn Avenue, Toronto, Ontario, Canada M4V 3B2
Penguin Books (N.Z.) Ltd, 182-190 Wairau Road, Auckland 10, New Zealand

Penguin Books Ltd, Registered Offices: Harmondsworth, Middlesex, England

First published in the United States of America by Puffin Books,
a division of Penguin Books USA Inc., 1994

1   3   5   7   9   10   8   6   4   2

Copyright © Candy Dawson Boyd, 1994
All rights reserved
Library of Congress Cataloging-in-Publication Data
Boyd, Candy Dawson.
Fall secrets / by Candy Dawson Boyd.   p. cm.
Summary: In the aftermath of the 1991 firestorm in Oakland, California, sixth grader
Jessie enters a performing arts middle school where she pursues her dream of becoming
an actress and struggles with feelings of low self-esteem.
ISBN 0-14-036583-4
[1. Schools—Fiction.   2. Acting—Fiction.   3. Performing arts—Fiction.
4. Self-acceptance—Fiction.   5. Afro-Americans—Fiction.   6. Oakland
(Calif.)—Fiction.]   I. Title.
PZ7.B69157Fal   1994   [Fic]—dc20   94-10921   CIP   AC

Printed in the United States of America

To my one and only sister, Stephany

chapter 1

I will win. I'm ready. Wait until they see me. I'm ready. I am. . . . I'm ready. Jessie Williams, you are the best. Remember to sit deeply and breathe straight. No, that's wrong. Sit straight and breathe deeply, Jessie frantically reassured herself.

"Miss Williams, please take a seat here," said a tall, bearded man.

Jessie Williams crossed the fingers on both hands for good luck. With more panache than she felt, she stood up and sat down before a committee of teachers and students.

"Good morning," Jessie said, tilting her square chin up, careful to speak distinctly. She watched the black man take his seat and arrange a pile of papers into a neat stack. *One strong wind and they'd blow all over this little theater.* Jessie swallowed a nervous giggle at the thought.

"Good morning. I'm Mr. Reynolds, head drama teacher. The rest of the committee will introduce themselves to you during the interview. Now, Miss Williams, please tell us about yourself and why you want to be a student at the Oakland Performing Arts Middle School."

Two of the other three members leaned forward. Jessie eyed the older girl on the end, posed in her chair like a movie star. She swallowed.

"My goal is to become one of the best dramatic actresses in the history of stage and film. I have worked in the theater since I was four years old. You have my application. You know that my grades are good and that I am very serious about this. Oakland Performing Arts Middle School is the *only* place for me," Jessie emphasized, trying hard to ignore the girl's lifted eyebrows. "What else would you like to know about me?" Jessie's dark eyes flashed.

A woman spoke up, her voice deep and melodious. "Why are you so serious about theater?"

Jessie answered, "Because I love to act! Being someone else, learning their story, and then acting it out, that's a whole world of its own, a world I love! Besides, there aren't nearly enough African-American dramatic actresses. I intend to change that. When I am old and wealthy and retired, I want to start a drama school and train young girls like I was—I mean, like I am now."

For a few long seconds the committee was silent.

"Do you have any sisters or brothers? Any hobbies?" asked the girl on the far left end.

Jessie cringed. *Now why would this particular black girl, with her straight hair and light skin, ask me about my sister of all things? And she looks a lot like Cass to boot. Well, this girl just met her match.*

Faking a friendly smile, Jessie asked, "And your name is . . . ?"

The girl tossed her hair and crossed her arms. "Sylvia Duncan. This is my last year at OPA."

Jessie grinned. "Hi, Sylvia. I have a wonderful older sister, Cassandra, who's a real inspiration to me. She'll be a senior at Oakland High." Jessie thought quickly. "And my major hobbies include chess, soccer, modeling, and downhill skiing."

Sylvia blushed. Mr. Reynolds cleared his throat. An elderly woman, her hair the color of soft white paint, chuckled. Her gray eyes fixed Jessie to the chair.

"Jessie, my name is Sonya Winston. So, my dear, you want to become part of theater lore. Well, you certainly come from theater. Your grandmother must be an inspiration for you," she said. "Her repertory company enjoys an outstanding national reputation."

Suddenly, Jessie became aware that somewhere behind her Mamatoo, her grandmother, had heard every single word she had uttered. *Uh-oh.* This was the wrong time to show off. *Mamatoo said tell the truth. No trying to impress them. No acting. Just be Jessie Williams.*

"Thank you, Mrs. Winston. I am very proud of my grandmother and I want her to be proud of me. Getting accepted here is important to me. I promise that I'll do my best."

"I'm sure you will, Jessie," said Mrs. Winston.

When Mr. Reynolds asked her to go up on the stage and present the piece she had prepared for the audition, Jessie's confidence wavered. She lifted her chin and focused her mind on the famous speech she had rehearsed for months. Jessie willed herself to climb the stairs. The theater was eerily silent. She walked to stage center and faced the committee.

But they had been replaced by a crowd of angry people packed in a large speaking hall. It was 1851. No longer Jessie Williams, she was in Akron, Ohio, at a women's rights convention. Illiterate, mother of thirteen children, she leaned forward to hear the speakers arguing against rights for women better.

As the angry voices swelled, she felt the spirit move through her. She stood. Dressed in a plain black dress and bonnet, she followed the light of the sun to the speaker's platform. A small, dark-skinned woman, she stuck out in the crowd of white people. Uninvited and unwelcome, she defied hostile, wary faces.

A surge of energy shot up her spine. The will that gave her the courage to flee from slavery twenty-five years ago gave her the breath to speak out. Someone had to speak for the women and children laboring in cotton fields under the whip. Someone had to stand up for the more than fifty million Africans who had perished during the nightmare of the Middle Passage. Someone had to do battle with ignorance and evil. Who better than she?

Sojourner Truth spoke. The spontaneous words flowed out. In the midst of the crowd, she spotted the one man whose words had pierced her like the cold of the old, wet cellar in Ulster County, New York. For a moment she remembered the long, bitter years in that cellar—her family forced to live there by the people who owned them. She shook her head. That was then. Now she could speak out.

"My name is Sojourner Truth. The Lord gave me *Sojourner* because I was to travel up and down the land showing the people their sins and being a sign unto them. Afterwards I told the Lord I wanted another name, 'cause everybody else has two names, and the Lord gave me *Truth* because I was to declare the truth to the people."

Sojourner Truth paused, ignoring the hoots and boos from the crowd. Her voice rose up and she pointed her finger at the man. "That man over there says women need to be helped into carriages, and lifted over ditches, and to have the best place everywhere. Nobody ever helps me into carriages, or over mud puddles, or gives me any best place. And ain't I a woman? Look at me! Look at my arm! I have ploughed and planted, and gathered into barns, and no man could head me. And ain't I a woman? I could work as much and eat as much as a man—when I could get it—and bear the lash as well! And ain't I a woman? I have borne thirteen children and seen most of them sold off to slavery, and when I cried out with my mother's grief, none but Jesus heard me! And ain't I a woman?"

Conversations ceased. Wary eyes watched her. Sojourner Truth's strong, rough voice rolled on. At last, fatigued, she uttered her final sentence: "Obliged to you for hearing me, and now old Sojourner ain't got nothing more to say."

The sound of her grandmother clapping brought Jessie back to the drama theater and the hushed committee. She lowered her head the way Mamatoo had taught her, waited briefly, then exited stage right. Mr. Reynolds thanked her. She would receive their decision regarding her admission status by August first.

Exhausted, Jessie closed her eyes and took a deep breath. That meant a wait of seven weeks. The Oakland Performing Arts Middle School received hundreds of applications. But only the best got accepted.

For seven weeks, Jessie sat on pins and needles. When an envelope bearing the name of the school arrived, she opened it slowly. Silently, she read the contents and handed it to Mamatoo, her grandmother and drama coach. The moment she'd been living for had come, but Jessie couldn't accept it at first.

"Is it true, Mamatoo?"

Her grandmother nodded her head. Early afternoon sunshine highlighted the golden strands woven into the African cloth turban she wore.

Chapter One

"I made it. They want me! Me!"

"You bet they do!"

Miss Jessie Williams was now a sixth-grade student majoring in dramatic and theater arts at the famous Oakland Performing Arts Middle School. The school's reputation of twenty years blazed across her brain like Halley's comet. Several of the nation's most acclaimed actors, painters, dancers, and musicians claimed the school as their first artistic home.

Jessie smiled, remembering the audition and that thrilling morning in August when she had opened the long-awaited letter. Now it was September. Summer was over. Outside, the early evening fog crept toward the redwood house in the Oakland hills where Jessie's family lived. Chilly, damp air signaled the end of summer.

Inside the house, Jessie made a face at herself in the bedroom mirror. Disgusted, she unbuttoned the blue jeans dress and tossed it on her bed. Nothing looked special enough for her first day at the Oakland Performing Arts Middle School tomorrow.

Jessie caught her reflection in the floor-length mirror. With skin the rich color of dark gingerbread and dark, shoulder-length hair, she stood long and lean. In less than twelve hours, she would be starting her first day at OPA. Biting her bottom lip, Jessie rummaged through her closet. Her favorite pair of blue jeans lay in a corner. Jessie snatched them up.

"I need good luck tomorrow," she muttered to her-

urned, opened a clothes drawer, and riffled
le of T-shirts. At the bottom of the second
pile, she paused. This was it. Her lucky red T-shirt,
worn and a bit stained, was exactly what she needed.

"Hey, want to come upstairs and play Scrabble with
us? Me and you against Dad and Mom?" Cassandra
sauntered into their bedroom. "Oh, no! Don't tell me
you're going to wear that on your first day? Jessie, you
can't be serious!"

"Cass, leave me alone. When I want your fashion advice, I'll ask for it." Clutching the T-shirt, Jessie faced
her older sister. Not only was Cass a senior in high
school, she was a beautiful senior in high school, a
cheerleader, and an honors student.

"Jessie, do I look like a child? I have spent years
learning about how to look good. I know how to do
hair, make-up, accessorize, and dress. Look at me! I
know how to help you."

Her sister's hazel eyes widened. She tossed her
straight, long hair. Cassandra Williams was a cream-
colored African-American, fair-skinned like their father, while Jessie was the image of their dark-skinned
mother.

"You look the way you always do, like a model,"
Jessie said, throwing the T-shirt on her bed.

"Jessie, don't start that. You are too pretty to wear
that old shirt. And, oh, no, not those jeans! Why don't
you wear that deep blue blouse with your *new* jeans?
I'll lend you my blue lacquer earrings. Blue is your
color."

Color. Jessie touched one dark brown hand. In her mind, she saw eyes the same color. She glanced at her sister. Strangers always seemed surprised when they learned that she and Cass were sisters. Jessie knew why. They didn't resemble one another—at least not in terms of their skin color and hair texture. Her hair wasn't straight like Cass's, but somewhere between nappy and curly. *We look like day and night.* Unconsciously, she touched the skin on the back of her hand again.

"I don't want to wear any earrings tomorrow." Jessie retreated to the large window facing the bedroom door.

Beyond the house, the landscape was bare. Stick trees, a few brick chimney stacks, and scorched earth stood as bleak testaments to the horrific fire that had consumed over three thousand homes and apartments in the Oakland and Berkeley hills, less than a year ago.

Jessie shivered. She'd never forget the terrible fire that had nearly destroyed their home. On a Sunday in October, houses and apartments in the hills of Oakland and Berkeley, California, had burned to the ground at a rate of four hundred per hour.

Twenty-five people had been killed, ranging in age from eighteen to eighty-five years old. More than two hundred people had been injured, some badly burned. Ravaging sixteen hundred acres of land and jumping freeways, the fire had raged, out of control, for hours. Families had witnessed the destruction, watching the fire burn everything they cherished. Houses and cars had exploded.

"I can still feel that hot, strong wind. And smell the stink of the thick, black smoke. Everywhere," whispered Jessie. "The sky was so dark, like midnight. Except for the flames, those huge flames shooting up."

Cass moved to the window, caught up in the memories of that time. "Me, too. I thought the sky was falling in. It happened so fast. One minute we were planning to go to the movies and the next minute, fire was burning up the trees outside this window, and Mom was shouting at us to get Mamatoo and grab clothes and photographs! So much noise! People yelling! The planes and helicopters!"

"And Dad was throwing the ladder against the house. Mom scrambling to get him the garden hoses. Mr. and Mrs. Caldwell hosing down their roof and yard, over and over. Mrs. Yashima calling for that crazy old cat Roxie, while Mr. Yashima tossed their stuff into green garbage bags to get it all out of there. Oh, Cass, then when they found Roxie, she was dead."

"I know, Jess, I know," Cass soothed. "Jess, it's hard for me to believe that Mom actually pushed us in the car and drove off. I mean, there was Dad, alone in the fire, on the roof, trying to keep it wet so the house wouldn't burn."

Jessie turned toward her sister. "Cass, Dad refused to leave. He forced us to leave him. Mom yelled and screamed at him to get off the roof, but he ignored her. He made her get us out of there. You know that."

Tears fell down both of their faces.

"I know, Jess. Mom cried all the way down the hill. Poor Mom. Crying and driving. Mamatoo kept praying, saying that the Lord would take care of Dad."

Jessie slid the bedroom window open.

"When we first saw Dad afterward, we didn't even recognize him."

"He was covered with soot and ash. And that bad burn on his hand and arm . . ." Cass stopped, too choked to continue.

Jessie nodded. "But Dad saved our house and the Yashimas'."

"He could have died," Cass insisted.

Jessie finally spoke up. "Cass, if Mom or Dad had made even one tiny mistake or if a car had stalled in front of us, or if we just hadn't been lucky, we could have died too."

Jessie had known the kids who'd come to school a few weeks later with real-life nightmares to tell. Books, toys, furniture, family albums, art, clothes, even pets—gone. Her teacher had explained that hundreds of dogs and cats were missing, probably alive but roaming hungry, scared, and lost, maybe even badly injured. Pets, books, photographs, toys. Memories. Her classmates no longer had homes, addresses, or telephone numbers. Not even mailboxes.

Only the arrival of a fire truck, a shift in the wind, and Dad's refusal to leave had saved their home. Jessie shook her head to blur the image of Dad on the roof with the garden hoses spewing water. His face scorched from the heat of the fire. Jessie had read that at times the fire had been two thousand degrees Fahrenheit, melting metal, even making mirrors turn liquid and run together. The memory of Dad standing on that roof throughout the day and night was too scary for her to bear. He never discussed the fire. Never. But she and Cass still did.

Every so often, Jessie and Cass managed to find some private time together to talk about the fire. Just being able to share what they had seen and heard and felt during those nightmarish hours made them feel less frightened. Somehow, each time they faced that time, together, a little of the terror left. *Like going to church*, Jessie thought. *When Reverend Brooks preaches about the bad times, some people wave their hands or cry. Especially when the choir sings. But when we leave church, we feel better and stronger.*

Inescapably, Jessie's mind drifted back to the day of the fire. She heard people shouting, trees exploding, fire engines, airplanes, and helicopters blaring out "Evacuate! Evacuate immediately!" She saw adults running down the hill. Children wailed and screamed. Sometimes Jessie still heard them in her dreams.

It had been so hot. So hot. The fire had stalked the hills like a wild beast, consuming everything in its path, leaping from one place to another. Jessie held her head.

"I know, Jess. I can't forget it. I even dream about it." Jessie felt her sister's arms surround her. "But we have to remember that the fire was last year. And tomorrow, my sister, the actress, soon-to-be-star, makes her entrance at the Oakland Performing Arts Middle School. I am really proud of you, girl. Now come on out and play Scrabble with us. You need to take your mind off tomorrow."

Jessie edged away. Her feelings tumbled about like clothes in a dryer. "Cass, I need to get ready. I don't want to play Scrabble right now, okay?" Jessie tried to be gentle. Even so, there was pain in Cass's eyes as she left the bedroom.

Jessie carefully hung up the clothes on her bed. What to do now? What would tomorrow be like? Jessie knew whom she needed to talk to. From the stairway to her left that led up to the living room, her father's grumbles and her mother's laughter told her that Mom was winning.

It was easy to sneak past them. That was one thing she liked about this house. The living room, dining room, a study, bathroom, and even the kitchen were all located upstairs on the first level. Everything else was downstairs on the lower level.

Down the hallway, past the bathroom and the laundry room, Jessie stopped. At the end of the hallway stood a solid wooden door. She pushed the buzzer above the light switch four times, once long, then short, short, short. When the door opened, Jessie rushed in, crossing the room quickly. Without pausing, she threw herself onto the sofa. Sandalwood incense burned in a holder on the end table. A fire crackled. Soft lights warmed the room.

"So, another dramatic entrance. What am I going to do with you, child? No, don't tell me—you said something mean to Cassandra and now you feel guilty. I'm making myself a cup of camomile tea. Can I brew you a mug of hemlock?" Clucking, Mamatoo patted her granddaughter's shoulder.

Jessie buried her head in the soft pillows. Moments later, she dragged herself up. A counter sliced off the rear of the long room. The room took up about half of the bottom floor of the house. Behind the counter a small woman dressed in a beautiful red velour robe poured boiling liquid into a mug. She handed it to Jessie.

"Don't worry, it's not hemlock, just hot cider. Get that plate of fruit," she said.

"Mamatoo, I'm going to explode. All I was doing was getting ready for school tomorrow. Cass came in and got on me about wearing my old jeans and the T-shirt you bought me that time we went to see *Dreamgirls*. Remember?"

"That was years ago. That T-shirt deserves the rest that comes with work completed above and beyond the call of duty. Child, I wouldn't wear that T-shirt to my worst enemy's funeral."

Jessie giggled. "I know, Mamatoo. But it's my good-luck shirt. I wore it under my dress when I auditioned. You even told me it would help."

"Now, you know that I'll say whatever it takes to get a good performance out of an actress."

Both of them smiled. They shared the world of theater. Mamatoo was the artistic director of a repertory company in Oakland. Jessie's shoulders dropped. Her grandmother on her mom's side had moved in two years ago, after the death of her second husband.

Mamatoo reached for her teacup. Jessie saw the tremor in her right hand. She wanted to reach over and will it to stop. But she knew that Mamatoo would not allow that. Not one to feel sorry for herself, last July Mamatoo had calmly announced to the family that she had been diagnosed with a mild case of Parkinson's disease. Jessie heard the rest of what Parkinson's disease meant reverberate in her head. No pain, but the disease was incurable.

"Jessie, stop staring at my hand. There you go again, chewing over something that you can't do a thing about. You know the doctor said that if I ate a healthy diet, exercised, and kept the stress low, I could live a full, normal life."

"I know. I couldn't live if anything happened to you, Mamatoo," wailed Jessie.

The elderly woman set her teacup down.

"Jessie Williams, I won't have hysterics around me. Now, let's discuss what's really got your corn popping. Besides being twelve years old," she said, leaning back in the beige easy chair.

"I'm . . . scared. Going to a performing arts school.

Starting middle school. Leaving all my friends. I'm not like Cass. She makes friends right away. Everybody likes her. She's beautiful." Jessie whispered the last word.

"And smart and a cheerleader and she's going to be a pediatrician," stated her grandmother, directing each word individually at Jessie. "And she loves you very much, and she did not ask to be born light-skinned like her father and me with hazel eyes and straight hair. I've told you time and time again that we are a rainbow people. African-Americans come in all shades of blacks and browns and creams—just like our family. When you celebrate your beauty, I'll rejoice. I wish I knew what makes you feel this way about yourself. You weren't always like this."

Jessie gazed off. She had only been in fourth grade the day the terrible thing happened. On that rainy afternoon, she had learned that somebody you admired, even loved, could believe that you were ugly and dumb. Not only believe it, but tell others. *No one knows what I heard that day. Not Dad, Mom, Cass, not even Mamatoo. If they knew, they'd understand. Not everybody believes that being dark skinned is good.* The old hurt sliced through Jessie like a sharp, new razor blade.

"Child, wipe that miserable expression off your face! How can I help you realize how beautiful and smart and talented you are? You are my joy, just like my daughter, your mother. I had to go through this with her and now you."

With effort, Jessie said, "I'm sorry. I didn't come down here to upset you."

"I'm not upset, just puzzled. I've been hearing you go on about Cass being so pretty because she's got light skin and you don't. Yet at the same time you went to OPA and gave a superlative performance as Sojourner Truth—a very dark-skinned woman who certainly wasn't considered even attractive." Mamatoo stared at Jessie. "No actress can do justice to a part that she does not understand. Part of you respects more than Sojourner Truth's intelligence and courage. Part of you sees her as beautiful."

"I hadn't thought about that, Mamatoo," Jessie admitted.

"Start using that head of yours for more than a place to grow hair on! What about your own mother? You look like her."

"Stop teasing me! Mamatoo, Mom is drop-dead gorgeous! People stare when Mom walks in a room! If I looked one tenth like Mom—"

Mamatoo threw her hands up in the air. "She is my daughter, and you resemble her more than you know."

Eager to change the subject, Jessie spoke up. "OK. I'll think about what you said, Mamatoo. Now, what should I wear tomorrow with my red T-shirt?"

At that, her grandmother laughed. "I am aware that Oakland Performing Arts Middle School means a major change for you. And the red T-shirt is only the tip of the iceberg."

"Mamatoo, I don't have any friends there. Plus at this school, we'll take different subjects and have different teachers. What if I don't fit in? What if nobody likes me? What if I try out for the plays and don't get a part? What if—"

"Enough, Miss What-If. What if you weren't going to the Oakland Performing Arts Middle School tomorrow? What if you looked just like Cassandra, without one single iota of acting ability? What if you found out that you'd spend the rest of your life as Dr. Jessie Williams, pediatrician, and not Jessie Williams, actress?"

Just then, the buzzer sounded. One long. Mom. After a nod from her grandmother, Jessie let her mother in.

"Where else would I find the two of you? Correct? Both of you huddled together down here? Mother, did you take your medicine? Can I get you anything? Jessie, why aren't you getting ready for school? Why does Cass look so unhappy? I feel like I'm in the demilitarized zone in a war." With that, her mother sank down on the sofa and swallowed some of Jessie's cider.

Jessie and Mamatoo exchanged a glance. Mom always asked a string of questions before she made a statement. Perhaps it was because she was a loan manager for a bank and had to ask questions for a living.

"Daughter, I surrender. Proceed to make me a dependent, weak, befuddled old woman unable to drink a drop of water without you holding the battered tin cup. I'll install a bell and ring it every time I take those darn pills. Will that make you happy?"

Jessie smothered a giggle. Watching the two of them was great theater. *Mom is so beautiful! I wish I looked like her, but that's impossible.* For twenty minutes Jess relished the exchanges that flew between two of the people she loved best. At last, Mom threw up her hands in defeat.

"Mother, it is no use trying to reason with you. Jessie, you've got to get ready for school. And your father wants to have one of his 'First Day at the New School Chats,' so show the proper respect." Mrs. Williams stood up, tall, ebony, and elegant. "I hope this helps you get your act together, Jessie. Your father and I want to see top grades again. Since fourth grade your grades have been uneven."

"But, Mom, I always end up doing well," protested Jessie.

"I know, you somehow manage to get decent grades by the end of the year, but only after we've put you on punishment. That won't fly in middle school. We have to see steady high-quality work with the same great grades you used to get. Hopefully, being at this school will motivate you," said her mother.

"There was the trauma of the fire, daughter," murmured Mamatoo.

"Mother, believe me we've made allowances for that," Mrs. Williams said. "But Jessie's work at school started sliding before the fire. And she had a marvelous fourth-grade teacher: Mrs. Grant! You remember her? She was simply the best. Cass had her, too, in fifth grade."

"I met Mrs. Grant, twice. She wasn't exactly my cup of tea. But that's beside the point." Mamatoo rested her head on the back of the chair.

"Oh, Mother, just because Mrs. Grant talked too much about what a delight teaching Cass had been. The point is that Jessie's grades have to reflect how smart she is. Understand, Jessie?" asked her mother.

Jessie sighed. Mamatoo's expression stopped her from doing more. She kissed her grandmother on the cheek and left. Taking the twelve steps two at a time, Jessie hurried upstairs. Her father was sitting in the living room. He gestured to her to sit next to him. Jessie stared out the sliding glass doors.

Their two-story home perched on a hill facing the San Francisco Bay. As with most homes that had a view of the bay, the back of the house consisted of more windows and sliding glass doors than regular walls, to increase the breathtaking view of bridges, water, and sparkling lights.

Jessie reflected. Buying the house two years ago had been both a sad and a happy event. Long ago, her grandparents on her father's side used to live in Denver, Colorado, but they regularly traveled back and forth for holidays. She recalled times rich with rousing conversations, laughter, gifts, and love.

Then Dad's father had passed away five years ago of complications from diabetes. So the death of his mother from a stroke only three years later had been a terrible shock. They had willed their only child, Jessie's father, a large inheritance to use as he saw fit.

Dad and Mom had decided to buy the house in the hills. They had paid cash for the house, investing the remainder of the money in a trust fund for their daughters' education. All of their lives had changed. Jessie frowned, wishing they could have stayed in their old neighborhood. She still missed her friends there.

This house was so different. The previous owners had used part of the floor space on the lower level to build a small one-bedroom apartment for their daughter. Now Mamatoo lived there.

A long redwood deck provided the ideal place to stargaze. Or it had before the fire. Now, blocks of burned empty lots destroyed any sense of tranquillity.

Jessie looked around the living room. Mom's taste ran to comfortable furniture, books, and plants. Skylights let in sunshine. Plants flourished. Dad's bookstore supplied most of the books. African-American art covered the walls. African sculpture peopled the shelves.

Jessie's eyes settled on her father. She clenched her hands. Her bespectacled father looked more worried than usual. He was light-skinned like Cass, and Jess saw dark circles under his eyes. Sales were down for many small businesses. But for a business that specialized in African-American books, cards, art, jewelry, and clothing, staying solvent remained a precarious undertaking even in the best of economic times.

The slightest falloff in sales distressed him. He knew that the success rate for African-American–owned businesses was poor. Far too many middle-class

African-Americans chose to spend their book and art dollars at stores elsewhere, not at stores owned by their own people. Jess had heard her father and mother talk about this many times. But something bothered her. *I wonder why he says all that, but moved us out of our black neighborhood, up here to the hills, away from all of our friends. I don't understand him sometimes.*

Dad had bought the store fourteen years ago. Located in downtown Oakland, not far from the convention center, the bookstore continued to make a profit, supported by loyal customers, black and white. But her father never stopped worrying.

"Now, Jessie, tomorrow is a brand-new beginning for you. Are you prepared for the challenges?" he asked, keen eyes pinning her to the chair.

"Yes, Dad." She tried not to focus on the scars on his hand. He had full use of his right hand, but the fire had left a permanent scar.

"Excellent. Your record hasn't been up to par the last two years. I don't understand what's going on with you, Jessie. We didn't go through this with Cassandra. I don't think that this acting plan of yours is very practical, but . . ." He paused and put his hands together.

Jessie interrupted, "Dad, my dream is to be a dramatic actress."

"I want you to concentrate on your studies, and if this acting bug helps you do that, then I'll go along with it. But if I don't see strong, consistent improvement in your grades, you go into a regular middle school," he said.

"I can't go to a regular middle school! I'll do whatever it takes to stay at OPA."

"We'll see. Jess, I am serious about this. Now, you know the rules. They stay the same. No boys over, no dating, top grades, no drugs, alcohol, cigarettes . . ."

Jessie struggled to seem attentive as he recited the usual list. There were times when her acting ability came in handy. Cass endured the same speech at the start of every school year. Except for the boys and dating. Cass had a handsome boyfriend.

Dad meant what he said. There was no room for mistakes. Finally, he stopped and kissed her cheek. Jessie returned the affectionate gesture and headed downstairs.

Cass was in bed, her back to Jessie's side of the room. From the set of Cass's back, Jessie knew that her sister was awake. Once under the covers, Jessie turned off the light. But no matter how hard she tried, she couldn't calm down enough to fall asleep. She realized part of what was troubling her.

"Cass, I'm sorry. Thanks for trying to help me," she said. Silence answered.

"Cass."

"You're welcome. Don't worry, Jessie, you'll do fine tomorrow."

Jessie grinned.

During the night she tossed and turned. At some point, she jerked up, sure that the house was aflame. It wasn't. Careful not to disturb Cass, Jessie tiptoed out. Her parents' bedroom door was shut. She moved like a cat, climbing each stair with grace. The night light in the kitchen was on.

With a glass of milk and a peanut-butter-and-banana sandwich, Jessie settled on the couch. Fog clung to the deck. She pulled the woolen throw around her and enjoyed her snack.

Later, when she was back in bed and snug, Jessie's mind swirled. Tomorrow was here. *Can I get the grades that Dad wants? Will I make friends? Should I wear the blue blouse? Will the seventh and eighth graders make fun of me? Do I have what it takes to be an actress? What if I fail?* Slowly Jessie drifted off to sleep, wishing that she had the confidence and courage that made Sojourner Truth so beautiful.

chapter

2

After hugs from Mamatoo, a thumbs-up sign from Cass, and a smile from her father, Jessie eased into the front seat, and Mrs. Williams started the Volvo station wagon. Jessie would take the bus home. But this was a special day. Mom insisted on driving her.

"So, are you ready, Jessie?"

"No, Mom! I didn't sleep much."

Her mother laughed. "Honey, that's normal. You'll do just fine. You're smart, talented, and lovely. You know, you look like me when I was your age."

Jessie stared at her mother. "Mom, how can you say that?"

"Because it's true. You've got my long legs and facial features. And my skin color and hair. In time, you'll see what I see. Trust me, honey," said her mother.

As Mrs. Williams maneuvered the automobile around sharp, winding curves, Jessie practiced deep breathing. She tried to ignore the fire-scarred land around her. It would be many years before the hills were green again. Jessie's thoughts shifted. In only minutes she would be at her new school. Knowing that Mom worked less than a mile from the Performing Arts Middle School helped.

At least I'll have someone close by, she thought, as they approached the school. Her stomach cartwheeled and backflipped.

The Oakland Performing Arts Middle School was built on a large section of land located on the Oakland/ Berkeley border below the hills. The two-story, tan stucco building was deceptively small. Over five hundred students filled its rooms and corridors. Inside, the hub of the school contained the administrative offices, bathrooms, a large lunchroom/auditorium, two gymnasiums, a swimming pool, a separate teaching auditorium, the main library, and computer rooms.

There were four large wings. Three of them were called academic houses, one for each grade. The fourth wing contained classrooms, storage areas, dance rooms, the arts library, practice rooms, studios, and two small performing arts theaters. Donations from wealthy alumni, well-attended fund-raisers, and grant funds augmented the school budget. Up-to-date equipment and resources were plentiful.

Jessie made her way down the sidewalk toward the

front entrance. Everyone acted so grown-up and self-assured, calling to one another and laughing. Wide-eyed, anxious, darting glances gave the sixth graders away. Jessie hitched her book bag higher on her shoulder. The new blue jeans and turquoise blouse looked attractive, especially with Cass's pretty earrings. But underneath her finery, Jessie wore her lucky T-shirt.

The interior of the school pleased Jessie. White walls bordered in a sunny shade the color of apricots were alive with huge murals of dancers, musicians, singers, actresses, actors, and painters. She remembered them from that June audition morning. Figures leaped, played, and posed about her. Newly painted sky-blue lockers lined the halls.

Jessie followed guiding letters and numbers toward Academic House A, Room 114. Groups of students milled around her. Some were African-American. But others were white, Asian, Latino, and Indian. They joked together like close friends. Jessie frowned. That hadn't been the way it was in her old elementary school. There kids, especially older ones, kept to their own ethnic group.

Jessie hurried past the large, open library and turned right into the academic house for sixth graders. Two doors to her left, she spotted her Home Base room. The same tall, bearded man who had been on the interview committee was standing at the door, greeting each student.

"Well, good morning, Miss Williams. I'm Mr. Reynolds. You have me for Family Hour, humanities core, and improvisation and reader's theater," he said, holding out his hand.

"You know my name?" Jessie asked, shaking his hand.

"Jessie, how could I forget you? You knocked us out with your performance of Sojourner Truth. I look forward to being your teacher."

Smiling, Jessie went in. She saw a repeat of the white and apricot color scheme enhanced by posters of famous plays and performers. Shelves of books lined one wall. Sunlight streamed in. Mr. Reynolds's desk stood in the far right corner. Tables and chairs arranged in a circle took up the floor space. She was pleased to see an overhead projector, video machine and monitor, and six computer/printer stations in the room.

This school is really fancy, she thought.

Selecting a spot on the far side near the windows, Jessie glanced around. Girls and boys wandered in. Mr. Reynolds entered, closing the door behind him. Quickly, he took attendance and made notes as he called each name.

"Cooper, Addie Mae," he said.

"That's not my correct name. My name is Obidie Cooper," said a girl across the room from Jessie.

Mr. Reynolds pursed his lips. He started to say something and stopped.

"I see." He finished the roll. Jessie watched him eye the girl as he closed the attendance book. *What's the matter?* she thought.

"Welcome to your Home Base room and Family Hour. My name is Mr. Reynolds. We will convene here every morning and at the end of every day for thirty minutes. Your electives in your major will add another additional hour or so to your schedule," he said. "This makes for a longer day, but a rich one."

Then, he told them about himself. Married with two children, he had taught at OPA for eight years. He had a master's degree in theater and drama and wrote plays. When Mr. Reynolds described his experiences as a civil rights worker in the 1960s and 1970s working for Dr. Martin Luther King, Jr., and then Jesse Jackson, the class gasped. Jessie leaned forward, entranced. Her teacher was a hero!

"I teach at the Oakland Performing Arts Middle School because I want to. This is our Home Base room. Here we work to support one another and our community. We learn how to become a family," he said. Mr. Reynolds's eyes swept the circle of sixth graders. No one challenged him.

Then he had them count off: one, two, three, four, five, six. He directed all the Ones to make their own small circle and repeated directions for the other groups. Jessie was a Four. There were twenty-four kids in the room. Ten of them were boys. Jessie stood up. Three girls gazed about.

"Fours, over here. Get a move on. We work hard and we play hard," said the teacher, waving her over to them. "These are your permanent groups."

Jessie dragged her chair to the circle, listening as he

told them what to do. They were to share names, talk
about their families, goals, and one thing that frightened them. One person was to take notes. Another had
the responsibility of keeping time. The third member
was to lead the group, while the fourth student evalu-
ated how well everyone worked together. Mr. Reynolds added that the leader would be responsible for
introducing their team and summarizing what they had
accomplished.

"This man does not fool around. I'll be the leader.
Why don't you keep time?" said the light-skinned
African-American girl who had spoken up about her
name. "And you, take notes." She pointed to a white
girl, who checked her watch, and then to a girl who
looked Latina. "You, report on that working together
stuff."

She sure is bossy, Jessie thought, aware that this girl
had ordered her to report on the way the group cooper-
ated.

"First off, like I told Mr. Reynolds, my name is not
Addie Mae Cooper. My real name is Obidie Cooper. It
is pronounced, oh-BEE-dee-eh. It's a Nigerian female
name that means, 'Father's beloved child.' I live with
my mother . . ." Obidie hesitated. "And my father.
That's all."

"We're supposed to tell more," Jessie prodded, her
gaze fixed on this thin but muscular girl with plaited
hair, tawny-colored skin, and deep-set black eyes.

Obidie's words rushed out. "Both of my parents love

me a lot. I am a proud African-American. This school has one of the best dance programs in the state. My goal is to be a famous dancer like Judith Jamison and join a national African-American dance company."

"And what are you scared of?" pressed Jessie.

Addie Mae/Obidie Cooper's earrings and African jewelry clinked. She wore her hair in lots of long braids. Strands of her hair stuck out because it was too straight for a tight, finely braided style.

"Nothing. You go next," she ordered, pointing to the girl next to her.

Part of Jessie wanted to stick her tongue out at this bossy girl, but that would be childish. *I don't believe her. Everybody is afraid of something. Even me.*

"Wait a minute," said Jessie. "You have to be afraid of something."

"Why? Just because you say so? I have the right to share what I want to share when I want to. You go now," said Obidie, turning away from Jessie.

The white girl spoke in a soft voice. Small for a twelve-year-old, she had large brown eyes and short red hair. Even a face sprinkled with freckles could not conceal the sadness in her eyes.

I wonder what's the matter with her, Jessie thought.

"My name is Julie Stone. I live with my dad and mom and my brother, Mark. He's two years old. I play the violin. My parents thought that I should come here because . . ." Chewing on a nail, she paused and lowered her head.

"Because what?" demanded Obidie.

"Because it's a good school. A lot of things scare me. That's all I want to say." Julie looked away.

The dark-haired girl with a pencil in her hand stopped writing. "My name is Maria Hernandez. I am a Mexican-American and proud of it, too. I live with my father and mother and two brothers, not too far from here. I always wanted to go to this school. This is my dream come true. My goal is to become a concert pianist. And I'm going to do it, no matter what anybody thinks. The only thing that scares me is how big OPA is, but I'll get used to that."

Jessie smiled. *Maria isn't afraid to speak up for herself. Good.*

"How's our time?" asked Obidie.

Julie Stone checked her watch. "We have seven more minutes."

"You're up," directed the leader, pointing at Jessie.

"My name is Jessie Williams. You can tell what I am. I live with my father, mother, sister, and grandmother. I learned about this school from my grandmother, who is a well-known theatrical director. I want to be an actress. And I also sing."

"And what are you scared of?" asked Obidie.

"Not one single thing." Jessie delivered each word like a hard right jab, using her acting ability. *I can't let her know what scares me. I'll show her who's the tough one here.*

Addie Mae rolled her eyes. "My, my. We need to

talk about how we worked together. But we have time to organize our group for the rest of the week. Maria, you can keep on taking notes and—"

Ready to boil over, Jessie stared at Obidie/Addie Mae Cooper. The thought of spending one hour of every school day with Miss Mouth felt like a life sentence.

"Who made you leader? Nobody here did! If we are going to be a group, then I think everybody should be equal," Jessie interrupted.

"Hey, why not take turns? Jessie, you could be leader tomorrow," Maria said.

"I don't need to be leader. I just don't like her telling us what to do just because she thinks she can!"

Obidie's face flushed red. "Why waste five minutes deciding who is going to do this or that? Somebody needed to take charge. I don't have time to waste."

Jessie shook her head. "You could at least ask. Didn't your parents teach you any manners? You start taking over and deciding who talks and who does what. What's wrong with you? You think you're better than me?" Jessie wanted to snatch those last words and stuff them back in her mouth. Any black girl who resembled Cass rubbed her the wrong way.

"I'd watch my mouth if I was you. Don't bring my parents into this. You don't know anything about them. I've got the best parents in the world. And, Jessie, don't start that mess about me thinking I'm better. I know exactly what that means. I'm just as black and probably a lot blacker than you are. Being black is not a matter of how dark you are," Addie Mae declared, her eyes brimming with tears.

Shocked, Jessie felt her anger flare and fizzle. *This is some weird girl. First she acts like a marine drill sergeant. Then she folds! What's going on with her? I know that I got mad, but I didn't say anything to make her blow up like that.*

"If you two are going to fight like this, there's no way we're going to do well this semester," Maria stated, her dark eyes flashing. "I'll tell what else I'm scared of. Poor grades. I can't get anything but the best grades and reports."

"Me, either," whispered Julie.

Jessie nodded. She stood on shaky ground, too.

Mr. Reynolds called time. The leaders introduced their group members. Despite herself, Jessie admitted that Obidie did a polished job of presenting their group. She even gave Maria credit for taking accurate notes.

When it came time for Jessie to report on how well the group worked together, she hesitated. *We did listen to each other. But this is one strange group. One girl who doesn't talk. Another one who talks too much. Two who have to do great at OPA like me. Shoot, I don't want us to look bad in front of the rest of the class.* Jessie gave her group a top rating.

The remainder of the period was taken up with locker assignments and reviews of programs. Mr. Reynolds was also their advisor and counselor. He reviewed their general schedules for the day, directing the students to examine their maps of the school and mark their rooms.

The school did not use buzzers. There were too many different schedules for classes. Some classes met for blocks of time every day or every other day. Others didn't. It was the students' responsibility to be where they were supposed to on time.

After a reminder that he would see them at the end of their first day, Mr. Reynolds dismissed them.

"Here we learn that the quality of our work defines us," Mr. Reynolds said as they left. "Now remember these words: Make it a good day!"

Jessie scanned her schedule for the semester: a daily block for the humanities core, the mathematics and science core, physical education and health, and beginning Spanish. Then two six-week electives: improvisation and reader's theater, and history of drama, followed by a four-week elective in exhibition self-assessment. Every other sixth grader's schedule was a little different, depending upon each one's artistic major.

Jessie was relieved that there was no grouping by test scores at OPA. Before, when her grades had started to fall, she'd been tracked in lower reading and math groups in fourth and fifth grades. Everybody thought she was stupid! The kids in the top groups had taunted her. But here at OPA each student was considered academically talented. She would even be in some classes with seventh and eighth graders!

Her old school had been great, until the beginning of

fourth grade. The memory of the day she overheard those terrible things returned. That day was a secret that would stay one. No matter what. Shaking herself, Jessie squared her shoulders and raised her head. OPA was a fantastic fresh start for her. Jessie headed for her first real class.

A few minutes after she found the classroom, Mr. Reynolds walked in.

I hope he likes me. Or I could be in real trouble, Jessie realized.

Maria sat in a seat in the front. She gave Jessie a quick smile. Feeling better, Jessie smiled at her. The seats in the front were taken, so she chose one in the back corner.

The class listened as their assignments were explained. Addie Mae/Obidie Cooper ran in, out of breath. Jessie gritted her teeth. But when Mr. Reynolds passed out the core reading material—an anthology, two books for history, and three paperback books—Jessie forgot about Addie Mae Cooper.

Mr. Reynolds introduced the core theme, "Understanding ancient times helps us define ourselves today." Their literature and writing would be part of the theme. He reviewed the literature readings. By the time class ended, Jessie's head throbbed. *I'll need a bigger book bag. Shoot, I'll need a truck by the end of this day.*

The math/science core was worse. The class was larger, with two new teachers and another theme, "Understanding relationships and patterns in math and science helps us solve ecological problems." Seeing Julie in the class was a surprise. She sat absolutely still and quiet, showing little reaction to what was happening around her. That class piled three more books onto Jessie's load and a thick laboratory workbook that the math and science teachers had written.

By lunchtime, Jessie yearned to go home, climb into bed, and hide under the covers. With five chapters to read tonight, a short paper to write, a geometry problem set, and an ecologically friendly house to design, she'd need a miracle to be ready for the next day.

In the lunch line, she selected the food she wanted, paid for it, and tried to figure out where to go. Modern white cylinders hung from the ceiling at different heights, supplying light. Jessie saw rows of long brown fold-up tables. At the end of the lunchroom was a stage.

Cass told me to check where the older kids went, so I didn't take their places. Maybe I can find some of the kids from Family Hour. Mr. Reynolds said that we were supposed to be friendly to one another, thought Jessie.

She heard a familiar voice. "Jessie, you want to sit with us?"

It was Maria. Jessie had never been so relieved to see anyone in her life. Trying to act confident, Jessie walked to the table.

"Hi, Maria. Thanks," she said, sitting across from a mute Julie.

"Sure. We're Fours, right?" Maria smiled.

"Yeah, we are," Jessie replied, feeling better. "This place is nothing like the school I came from. They even have two soda pop machines and two snack machines here!"

The lunch period flew by. When Addie Mae joined them, out of breath, and chattering a hundred miles a second, Jessie ignored her. Julie responded only when Maria murmured something to her.

A weird crew, Jessie thought again. *I wonder if I can get reassigned to a better one.*

In physical education, Jessie spotted all three other members of her Family Hour group. There were seventh- and eighth-grade girls in the class. Jessie was good at volleyball. The teacher, Miss Shimoda, went through the requirements for attendance, participation, and dress. Class ended a half hour early two times a week, to make time for health. By the time Jessie left there she had an additional text and two more assignments for health.

Weaving through other students, Jess headed for Home Base. Somehow she stumbled. Her books scattered. Just in time, Jessie caught her balance.

"You OK?" asked a male voice behind her, as someone took her arm.

Turning around, Jessie saw an African-American boy whose face nearly took her breath away. He was very good-looking with huge sweet eyes, skin the color of honey, and a smile that made his eyebrows lift. His face was all sharp angles. He seemed tall and muscular for his age.

"Yeah. Thanks," said Jessie, trying not to gawk. He released her arm.

He neatly stacked her books and then handed them over. "So, what's your name?"

The floor dropped under Jessie's feet. A boy, an older boy, was talking to her, on her very first day!

"Jessie. Jessie Williams. I'm new. I'm majoring in theater and drama." Jessie flushed, knowing that she was babbling.

"My name is Jamar Lewis. I am in theater and drama, too. But I'm a double major, I like history. I plan to be a United States senator."

Jessie swallowed. "You're ambitious. My dad believes that's important. Thanks for the help."

Quickly, she turned away. Having a boy pay attention to her was new and unsettling. Cass was the one with boys calling and wanting to date her. *Not me. I have to do well or Dad will send me straight to Milton Middle School. No ifs, ands, or buts.*

Jessie scurried to her Home Base room. *I need a family after today. And a vacation and a Jessie clone who can come to school and do the classwork, so I can study drama. And get some sleep!*

Students slumped in their chairs. Surviving their first day at the Oakland Performing Arts Middle School had taken its toll.

"What's the matter with her?" Jessie asked Maria, pointing to Julie. The girl gripped the edge of her chair, her features stretched taut as a rubber band.

Maria shrugged her shoulders and black, silky hair

swung from side to side. Her olive-colored skin and striking features gave Maria every reason to act stuck-up, but she didn't. She whispered, "Julie's having a rough time."

Jessie said, "Maria, you never said you knew her. Why not?"

Maria looked away. "I don't know her real well."

"What do you know about her?" pressed Jessie.

Maria said, "Look, Jessie, if you want to know what's wrong with Julie, ask her."

Puzzled, Jessie withdrew. Addie Mae tiptoed in. Late, as usual. A rise in Mr. Reynolds's voice caught Jessie's attention.

"You work in the groups you were in this morning for the rest of this semester. No changes. Now, I want you to plan your group's project. The major assignment in your Family Hour class will be the planning, implementation, and evaluation of this project," he said, striding up and down the width of the room. "It will count as 60 percent of your grade. It has to be integrated with your humanities core theme and your majors."

Addie Mae raised her hand. "What kind of project?"

As the teacher explained, the class groaned.

"Less than a year ago, we had one of the worst tragedies in memory, the Oakland/Berkeley fire. It destroyed thousands of residences and killed people. There are still many families out there who need assistance. In ancient times, you will learn that there were many disasters. Cultures who helped one another survived. Those who did not, perished. Can you think of a way to help others that would incorporate a combination of art, music, dance, or theater? What about our senior citizens? Or the homeless?" His eyes raked the room. "What about young people like you?"

"What can we do about the fire? It's over," said a boy in the back.

At this, Julie rose. Jessie saw tears in her eyes. What was the matter with that girl? She watched her go up to Mr. Reynolds, whisper something, and leave.

The class discussed the idea of the project. They had less than two weeks to come up with a plan. The three girls from group four frowned. Julie returned.

Maria started. "I live around here. I only saw the fire on TV. But my aunt lived in the Parkwoods Apartments, which burned to the ground. She almost died," shared Maria. "She lives with us now."

Obidie said, "That's scary. My mother works at a hospital. She had some sad stories about people who got hurt in the fire. Mama has a friend who was renting an apartment in the hills and lost everything. In March, she moved back to North Carolina. My father is an Oakland fireman. He helped fight the fire. I'm proud of him. What about you, Jessie?"

But before Jessie could reply, Mr. Reynolds signaled that it was time to stop.

"Announcement time. Listen up. At the end of the month we have our back-to-school dance. I expect to

see everyone there. Being involved in schoolwide
events is also part of your group grade. Check the hallways for posters and signs about other events. This was
your first day at OPA and a good one. We'll have a year
of good days together. See you tomorrow morning, on
time, and prepared," said the teacher.

"A school dance? Oh, no!" said Julie.

Maria frowned. "I don't really want to go to a dance.
I don't have time."

Jessie and Obidie echoed Maria. "Me neither."

Maria laughed. "Finally we agree on something."

The girls hurried to their major performing classes.
Jessie glanced at her map and stuffed it into a book.
She ran to the performing arts wing. About thirty-eight
students sat in the small theater. She saw Jamar Lewis
a few rows ahead of her. As if he knew she was there,
he turned around and waved. Jessie nodded.

With eager eyes, Jessie took in the stage, the comfortable seats, the lighting booth in the back, the
speakers around the ceiling, and the small orchestra
pit. This was for real! A real theater! This was the place
where kids became stars! Onstage stood two theater
and drama teachers. One was Mr. Reynolds. As usual,
he'd managed to reach the room before Jessie. *How did
he do that?* she wondered.

"Good afternoon. I am Miss Baker. I work part-time
at the school, team teaching with Mr. Reynolds. I am a
professional actress and have trained at ACT, the
American Conservatory Theater," stated the woman.

Her short, spiky blond hair, dangling earrings, and faded blue jeans did not match the crisp precision of her words or her ability to project her voice far beyond the last row.

Jessie was impressed. Mr. Reynolds's next announcement startled her. Some seventh- and eighth-grade students would be working in this class as assistants. Tryouts for an improvisation and reader's theater performance were scheduled in one week. The performance would be presented to other students in the school.

A student sitting in the front raised her hand. "Excuse me, but what is reader's theater?"

"I should have explained that, and improv as well. Excuse me," said Mr. Reynolds. "Reader's theater is a special kind of theater that will help you focus on voice and presence. You will be given scripts. Select the character you want to read for. Audition. Those who are selected go into rehearsal. You'll sit on a stool with the rest of the cast and practice reading from the script. The performance will be just like the rehearsals— sitting on stools and reading the script. So, props, costumes, and lighting are kept to a minimum. Is that clear? Any questions?"

"You mean we just read? We don't act?" a girl asked.

"No, you'll be acting, but you'll have to rely on your voice, posture, and presence to give life to your character," he explained.

That's harder than having all the theater props to help

create your character, thought Jessie. *I hope she knows that.*

"Miss Baker, why don't you talk about improv?" said Mr. Reynolds.

"I'd love to. I love improvisation. Improvisation or improv is spontaneous acting. You are given a situation and without any preparation, you act. There are other variations. The best way to explain it is to do it. Sylvia, Mike, and Robin, come on up," she said, pointing to each advanced student.

Jessie leaned forward. Sylvia Duncan was the girl who had been so uppity at her audition.

"Sylvia, you and Robin are good friends. Mike has just transferred into OPA. You both like him. Mike, you like Robin. You three are at the back-to-school dance. Go." Miss Baker sat down.

For the next eight minutes or so, Jessie watched the three actors create a hilarious scene. She had to admit that Sylvia Duncan was very good. The class clapped when Miss Baker called time. They listened as Mr. Reynolds described the auditions for the reader's theater play.

Competition would be fierce. Going up against more experienced seventh- and eighth-grade theater and drama majors meant that Jessie would have to work hard to be ready. Copies of the reader's theater script were in the library and on computer disk. The story was titled *Mufaro's Beautiful Daughters* and had been created by a recently deceased African-American author/illustrator named John Steptoe.

I have to get a copy of that today. I never even heard of an African version of the Cinderella story, fretted Jessie.

A review of the course requirements was followed by another small group of seventh and eighth graders coming up on stage to review improvisation and reader's theater. Their talent impressed Jessie. Sylvia Duncan was adept at moving from humor to drama.

"Shoot, Sylvia didn't transfer," said a girl who walked in and plopped next to Jessie. She was older. "I can forget the lead."

"Why do you say that?" asked Jessie.

"You see the girl in front, in the red jumpsuit? That's Sylvia Duncan. She always gets the lead. Don't even bother to try out for the big parts," the girl advised. "Especially if you're new."

Jessie frowned. Giving up before she started was not her way. *Sure Sylvia Duncan is good. But I am too,* she thought.

After class, Jessie dashed to the library. Fortunately there were copies of the script still available for checkout. The lending period was one week. She read the script. The setting was a village in Africa long, long ago. The main characters were an older African man named Mufaro, and his two teenage daughters, Manyara and Nyasha. Nyasha was the kind, gentle sister. Manyara was a real meanie. Fascinated, Jessie followed the story of a great king searching for a wife.

The African version was different from the Cinderella story Jessie knew. Manyara wanted to be the new queen. She hated her sister and was willing to do anything to win the king. Both girls traveled to the city where the king lived but at different times. Their journeys turned into adventures when each met an old woman who offered important advice on how to gain the king's favor. This was going to be exciting!

Catching the bus was easy, but she almost missed her stop rereading the African tale, which had been adapted for the stage. A four-block walk remained. Below her, Jessie saw the city of Oakland, part of Berkeley, and the Bay Bridge. Sniffing, she realized how much she missed the spicy, earthy smell of eucalyptus trees. Along with the eucalyptus, Monterey pine and cedar trees, juniper bushes, and coyote brush had burned like torches, the plant oils feeding the fire enough to give it the fury to jump ten freeway lanes.

She sighed. First, the earthquake, on October 17, 1989, just two years before the fire. That 6.9 earthquake had tossed the Bay Area like a rag doll. When the powerful rolls and rumbles stopped, over sixty people were dead, hundreds injured, and almost six billion dollars of damage had been done. Jessie remembered it all too well. She'd been in the old house, alone.

Jessie remembered hiding under the dining room table away from any breaking glass. It had been hours before she found out if everyone was safe. Hours of watching the television, seeing part of the huge Bay Bridge collapse, and the upper deck of a freeway fall, crushing people in their cars below. Then there were little earthquakes after the big one, called aftershocks.

Jessie trembled, recalling the darkness of the house and the lonely, solitary wait. Just when she had begun to put that behind her, the firestorm had erupted.

Now the house was quiet. Jessie dropped her book bag. She poured milk and cut a healthy slab of chocolate cake. No noisy halls. No classes to find. No locker combinations to remember. No Addie Mae or Obidie or whatever that girl wanted to be called. Just a peaceful silence wrapping itself around her like a warm blanket. How could her whole life have changed in one day?

I don't know if my T-shirt brought me good luck today or not. I've got eons of homework ahead of me. Plus the play. Jessie chewed on a chunk of cake.

She heard the sound of a sputtering car engine. Jessie opened the front door.

"Mamatoo, I have to try out for this play in one week. I need your help. I never even heard of this story," Jessie said, taking two bags of groceries. "Did you know that there are hundreds of versions of the Cinderella story in the world?"

"Well, I can see that you are bursting with excitement. Child, you have sat on my mind all day. I don't have much time. I have to go back to the theater for rehearsals. Yes, I do know about Cinderella. Are you doing Steptoe's African version?" In the afternoon light, the vibrant colors from Mamatoo's turban and long dress sparkled.

Her grandmother was so smart.

"Yes! It's great! I am excited. But scared, too. There is so much work. I have to get good grades. I know Daddy will transfer me if I don't. And I almost forgot—Mr. Reynolds, my Home Base teacher, told us we have to go to a dance at the end of the month! A back-to-school dance! I've never been to a dance before!"

Mamatoo chuckled. "Dances are part of school life. Stop worrying so much. Of course you'll do well, Jessie. I'll help you with the script. Read it over and decide what part you want to try out for. Then we'll talk. How can you doubt yourself?"

Jessie had an answer. She knew her grandmother would scoff at it. Surviving until Friday would be a miracle. The idea of weeks and months of this routine frightened Jessie. As she headed for her bedroom, the day hit her like a tidal wave. Classes, new teachers, a project, an audition, that handsome boy, Jamar Lewis, and worst of all and nearly lost in the mountains of work and information that day, a back-to-school dance!

What a day! Why did I end up as a Four? Why not a Three, or Five? Maria's OK. But Julie and Addie Mae are two disasters. What are their big secrets?

She switched her book bag to her other hand. *I must do well. When Dad says he wants to see good grades or I go to a regular middle school, he means it.*

Jessie dumped the contents of her book bag on her bed. Before she started to work, she had to clean her desk, change clothes, and set the table for dinner. She set to work, shoving the dance, Jamar, and everything else as far away as possible.

chapter

3

By Thursday afternoon, Jessie was moving like a zombie. Her feet felt like bricks. As she struggled to fit her key into the lock, she collapsed against the door. Her book bag bulged with notebooks, texts, paperback books, and pens. Once in, Jessie dropped it and headed straight for bed. She kicked off her shoes and nestled under the covers. Moments later she was asleep. Hours passed.

"Jessie. Jessie. Wake up. Come on," said Cass.

Reluctantly, Jess lifted one eyelid. "Why? What's wrong with you?"

Cassandra sat on the side of the bed. She pushed back her hair and wound it in a coil. Dressed in a maroon-and-white sweater and short skirt, Cass could be a cover for a teen magazine.

"We had tryouts today. It's a new rule. Everybody

has to try out each year. I think I made the squad."
Cass sighed. "It's time for dinner. You look like a truck
ran over you, Jess."

"Yeah. A truck loaded with books, assignments,
teachers, a weird Home Base group . . . don't get me
started," said Jessie, stretching.

"You were little when I started middle school. For
the first two months, I came straight home and went to
bed." Cass managed a small smile. "I feel like doing
that now."

"You?"

Cassandra stood up. "Being a senior in high school
is no fun. I thought it would be. But all I get from everybody is pressure, pressure, pressure. Where am I
going to college? Can I score in the top five percent?
Do I want to go to Spelman, like Dad and Mom
want? Atlanta, Georgia, is a long way away. And what
about—"

Alert now, Jessie finished the sentence. "Joe."

Frowning, Cass nodded. "We've gone together
for—"

"Two years and eight months. I forgot the number
of weeks and days. I used to keep count," admitted
Jessie.

Cassandra stared at her. "No. You're wrong. It's only
been a year and a half."

"Cass, I heard you sneaking to call Joe over a year
before that. I read what you wrote in your diary. So
don't try to fool me."

"You were reading my diary?"

"Sure. It's been one of my best sources for how not to grow up," teased Jessie. "I haven't been able to find it for the past five months. Wherever you hid it must be good."

Cassandra sputtered and swallowed air. "Why are you telling me this now? I suspected something. What about my right to privacy?"

"Don't get upset, Cass. What's a big sister for? Frankly, your diary bored me. Daddy doesn't have a thing to worry about. Poor Joe. I bet you haven't even kissed him good yet." Jess swung her legs around and touched the carpet.

"I share my personal problems with you and what do you do? Ridicule me! I don't know why you hate me, Jess." Two fat tears tumbled from her sister's hazel eyes.

Flabbergasted, Jessie grabbed her arm. "Hey, Cass, I didn't mean anything. Look, who can I tell? Why would I tell? I admit it, imagining you having problems is hard for me. Why? Dad loves you a lot more than he does me. You always do great in school. You'll be elected captain of the cheerleading squad, just like last year. You hardly ever break a rule. Come on, Cass, what do you have to cry about?"

"You're like everybody else. You don't see me, Jess. You never have. Not the real me. All you see is what you want to! Why did I ever think I could talk to you?" She ran into the bathroom across the hallway.

Jessie rubbed her forehead. *Shoot, I didn't mean to make Cass cry! What did I say to make her cry?*

Dinner was somber. Cass excused herself with an upset stomach. Mamatoo was at the theater. Dad seemed preoccupied. Mom yawned. Jessie picked at the spaghetti on her plate. She had three hours of homework to do. Plus, rereading the script was a must. *And that Family Hour project! Our time is running out.*

When Jessie got to Home Base the next morning, only Mr. Reynolds was there. She knew she was early. Hopefully, he would talk to her about the play.

"Morning, Jessie. You made it through your first week. How are you doing?" he asked, glancing up from a book.

"Fine. Well, that's not quite true, Mr. Reynolds. I pray I can make it to improv class." She paused, but he didn't interrupt. "I thought . . . it seems silly now . . . I know I got my course schedule, but I never expected to carry so many subjects *and* study drama."

"Jessie, you can't be a good, dumb actress. You'll use everything you are learning here and more as a professional. Believe me," he said. "Are you going to audition for *Mufaro's Beautiful Daughters*?"

"I want to. It's like Cinderella in some ways, but more unusual. I found the picture book. The illustrations should be in an art museum. I don't have much experience with reader's theater," Jessie admitted.

"You have to work harder than in other kinds of plays. Although you read your part, you have to give the character life without costumes, scenery, or stage lighting. Some people call it the Theater of the Mind."

"I like Nyasha and Manyara as characters. And the role of the narrator is a good one," she pressed, hoping for some direction from him.

Mr. Reynolds grinned. "Jessie, you've got talent in your fingernails. But you need maturity and opportunities to stretch that talent and learn your craft. My best advice is to go after the part that speaks to you, just like you did for the auditions that got you here."

Confused, Jessie thanked him. He had both praised her and informed her that she wasn't ready for the leading role. She didn't know whether to feel good or bad. Her group drifted in.

Mr. Reynolds called the roll. "Addie Mae Cooper."

Jessie waited for her to answer.

He repeated the name.

"Mr. Reynolds, I prefer to be called Obidie Cooper. That is the name I have chosen for myself," Addie Mae said.

"Do you know whose name you share?" he asked.

"Yes. My family is related to the Collins family of Birmingham, Alabama, on my mother's side. I know who I was named after," she stated.

"And you still prefer to be called Obidie?"

"Yes."

"You must have a powerful reason for not wanting to make that name live. I can't imagine what it could be."

She looked off, not meeting his eyes.

He shook his head. "Have it your way. Obidie Cooper?"

"Here, Mr. Reynolds."

Once they were in their groups, Jessie leaned into the circle.

"What was that about?"

Addie Mae glowered. "None of your business. Just call me by my name."

"I will. But why are you making such a big deal about your real name? Tell us what Mr. Reynolds is upset about," said Jessie.

"I don't want to be reminded of Addie Mae Collins. I want a name that fits me," said Addie Mae/Obidie. "Let me alone. I won't talk about this anymore."

"I hate to break in, but we have to come up with a community project. Sixty percent of my grade rides on what the four of us do," said Maria.

Jessie replied, "The closer to school, the better. What do you think, Julie?"

Julie sat quietly, one hand on her violin case. She carried it everywhere, except to physical education. Today her freckles stood out even more. Dark circles smudged the skin under her eyes.

"I agree, Jessie."

"We need to come up with someone to help and a way to help them," repeated Maria. "What's close by?"

Jessie shook her head. "No use volunteering to tutor the younger kids. We are the younger kids!"

Only Addie Mae didn't laugh.

"Let's brainstorm. I'll take notes," offered Jessie.

"What about lost pets or injured ones?" Julie offered.

Obidie snorted. "Come on, Julie! Mr. Reynolds told us to help people, not animals!"

Jessie saw Julie's face crumble, but she stood her ground. "There's a newspaper run by people who were burned out in the fire. It's called the *Phoenix Journal*. They think pets are important. There are articles in the newspaper and a place where you can go and see photographs of pets that have been found. Obidie, a lot of people got hurt when their dogs and cats were killed or missing."

"Yeah, yeah. OK, but I put people before pets," said Obidie.

"You can't talk to her like that, Obee, whatever your name is," said Jessie. "When you brainstorm, you accept every idea. No criticizing anybody."

"That's right," Maria echoed.

"OK. OK. And my name is not 'Obee-whatever.' It's Obidie. Remember that, Jessie," warned Addie Mae.

"Any more ideas?" Jessie ignored her.

At the end of ten minutes they had a list of twenty-six ideas. Seven came from Julie. Before they could whittle the list down, time was up.

Mr. Reynolds stood in front of the class. "I realize that this has been a tough, hectic week for you. But it's also been exciting and challenging. Focus on what is important and know that you always have Home Base. So, make it a good day!"

Friday raced by like a fast train. In her literature/history core class, Jessie delivered her report on ancient Egyptian pyramids. A quick dash to her locker and she grabbed her math/science project. Explaining how she had used the same shapes and dimensions to construct three distinctive houses that used solar energy went better than she thought.

Writing down her planning and thinking in her math journal helped. *I sure am glad I stayed up and reread the journal. There were important parts I forgot.* Jessie noticed that one third of the class was unprepared.

She spent her lunchtime at a computer, taking notes on material she had referenced from two electronic encyclopedias. As Jessie skimmed through the entries and ran off a diagram of the human heart, she reminded herself to talk to Dad about his diet. She shared her report with a group and handed it in. In Family Hour, they had to share their feelings about week one and their goals for the next week.

"Obidie, do you want to be leader?" Maria asked.

"No, I'll take notes."

"What about you, Julie? Everybody took a turn this week. I took two. All you have to do is to ask each of us to share," urged Maria.

"Who wants to share?" Julie asked.

Maria smiled. "I will. This week went fine. I like my classes, especially piano. We have tryouts for a series of casual performances called lunch-bag recitals in October and November. I hope I do well. I want to invite my parents. My goal for next week is for us to have a great plan for our community project. That's all."

"OK, who's ready to share next?" Julie asked gamely.

"I made a mistake coming to this school." Obidie's mouth tightened as she spoke up. "I came here to dance. I'm no beginner. I've been taking ballet, tap, and modern dance classes since I was five. But I still have to try out for a place in the African Dance Troupe. I'm better than most of them, any day."

Maria, Julie, and Jessie raised their eyebrows. Maria shook her head.

Now Jessie felt her own mouth tighten. "We all have to try out, no matter how great we think we are. You're no different. I don't like it, but that's the way it is at OPA. Come off it, girl. In my grandmother's repertory company, every actor has to audition every time."

"Look, Jessie, I came here to dance, not to do all this mess! So why are you here? Why aren't you at some fancy acting school?"

"You know what? Your mouth runs like a chain saw. My mother and grandmother were able to convince my father that it would be a good compromise for me to come here, instead of a regular college-prep middle school. Dad is tough. I mean, really hard on me. He'd never go for any 'fancy acting school.' So at OPA I get the academics he wants and I get to learn more about acting." Jessie folded her arms across her chest.

Addie Mae scrutinized Jessie. "Why call your father

tough? He cares about you. You should be glad for that."

"I know, but you try living with him! My folks hope that being at OPA will motivate me. Because of the fire. It almost destroyed our house and nearly killed my father. I started to go into a worse slump than—" Jessie stopped. There was no way she was going to tell this girl about that day in fourth grade. No way.

Everyone jumped when Julie knocked over her stack of books. Jessie helped her organize them.

"Thanks, Jessie." Julie smiled.

"What's your goal for next week, Obidie?" Maria asked.

"I wish next week would never come!"

"Look, Obidie. I came here to learn as much as I can about acting," Jessie said. "But by the time I get to the drama classes, I'm tired. If I want to stay here, I have to get top grades. My goal is to survive next week."

"I guess that leaves me," said Julie. "My folks really wanted me to come here, to help me . . . I don't want to talk about that."

"You don't have to," Maria said quickly.

Julie started again. "I like my music theory teacher. The orchestra class is exciting. But I don't expect to get a solo part or anything like that. I don't have a goal for next week. Just to make it here, I guess."

"We finished before time," Obidie said. "Any ideas for the project?"

"I have to say something. You and Jessie don't know what bad is." Julie's voice trembled. "I do. You don't know how lucky you both are."

Both girls stared at Julie.

In unison, they asked, "What are you talking about, Julie?"

"I'm talking about being grateful that you have a regular life."

"You don't know anything about my life! I wish it was the way it used to be. Every day I pray for it to change back." Suddenly aware of what she was saying, Obidie covered her mouth with her hand.

Just then, Mr. Reynolds called the groups together.

"From listening to your groups, it appears that you are managing to keep your heads above water! I'm proud of you. Now, remember we have fun at OPA too. The back-to-school dance is coming up. You'll get a chance to meet other students," he said. "Congratulations on a great week!"

Maria stared at Obidie.

Julie gathered her books and violin. "I wish Mr. Reynolds would stop bringing up that dance. Dances make me nervous."

"I've never been to one. Getting dressed up would be fun, but I don't know how my parents will feel about my going," Maria offered.

Obidie shrugged her shoulders. "Dances are stupid. I've got more important things to do."

"Well, for once I agree with you," said Jessie, looking at Obidie. "The last thing I want to do is to spend time at some dance. I'd rather be home sleeping."

Nodding, the girls filed out and headed for their major performance classes.

As Jessie approached the theater for I&RT class, which was what everybody called the improvisation and reader's theater class, she saw Jamar Lewis. Again, as if he sensed her presence, he turned and smiled. That had been happening all week long. Jessie's stomach flip-flopped. Someone pushed her aside. Jessie watched Sylvia Duncan push past her.

"Come on, Jamar! Follow me!"

With mounting anger and embarrassment, Jess watched the two of them walk in. Together. Laughing.

"Don't get upset. Hi. My name is River. My parents are into nature," explained the girl Jessie had sat next to on Monday. "Sylvia is always picking out the cutest boys, no matter what grade they're in. She does it just to show she can."

Jessie blushed. "He's not my boyfriend or anything like that. I don't even know him."

"You could have fooled me. You'll have your chance, don't worry. Sylvia drops them in a few weeks." River held the door open for Jessie.

Jessie wanted to hide under a rug. She hadn't realized that her feelings for Jamar were that obvious.

"I don't care about him, River, really I don't," Jessie stammered.

"Sure, and the sun rises in the south." River grinned.

Mr. Reynolds was beginning to explain the major exercise for that session. It was called "be a machine." The whole class would participate. No talking was allowed. Each student was to decide individually what part of the machine to be, select a place, and act out that part. Jessie bit her lip. This was another first.

One by one students took their places and began to move. Sylvia Duncan strode across the stage as if she owned it. She stopped right in front of Jamar Lewis. Facing him, she began to mirror his every move. Slowly, Jessie walked up. She moved to a space near the center of the human machine. With increasing energy, she pumped her arms and legs like a powerful engine.

As the machine grew, Jess forgot about Sylvia and Jamar. She was the heart of the machine. Her responsibility was to keep the parts running. In her mind, Jessie visualized the diagram of the human heart she had seen on the computer. Jessie concentrated on fueling all of the various rhythms of the machine. River had to shake her to stop.

Jessie laughed. "Oh! I love acting. I forget everything. It's like taking a vacation."

"You sound like the actress who came and talked to us last year," River said.

"Who was she?"

When River told her, Jessie gasped. "I saw her in a play in San Francisco. She's a real star!"

Buoyed by the exercise, Jessie enjoyed the rest of the class. As it ended, River gathered her books and stood up. "Have you decided what part you want to read for?"

"No! I like Manyara. She's not the nice sister, but she's dramatic."

River said, "Come on, Jessie. You can do better than that. What about Nyoka?"

"The snake?" protested Jessie.

They laughed.

"Jamar would make one fine king," River flung back as she left the theater.

"He sure would," Jessie murmured to herself.

But when Sylvia strolled out with Jamar in tow, Jessie flinched. *Even though he smiled at me, he left with her. This wouldn't happen to Cass.*

Friday evenings were a whirlwind for everyone except Jess. Dad kept the bookstore open late. Mom drove around getting errands done on her way home from work. Mamatoo worked overtime at the theater. And Cass got dressed to go out with Joe.

"So, what are you going to wear? Where are the two of you going?" asked Jessie, sprawled across her bed, observing her sister's preparations. The climate had been cool between them since their words earlier in the week. The gulf between them had widened since Thursday. This time Jessie knew an apology wasn't enough.

This wasn't the first time that had happened, for either of them. But for some reason, this time it bothered Jessie. She watched her sister. *Cass is my sister. Maybe she was right. Maybe I never see who she is, except in a disaster. We were closer during the earthquake and fire than we've ever been. Then she was my big sister first. I didn't think about how she looked. I was just glad to have her.*

Dressed in a terry-cloth robe, Cass pulled the steam-heated curlers out. Her hair tumbled to her shoulders in soft, bouncy curls. She took out nail polish and remover.

"We're going to the movies. I haven't decided what to wear. I get tired of feeling like I always have to look good. Maybe I should wear your lucky red T-shirt and jeans."

Jessie laughed. "Joe wouldn't care! You want to?"

Cass stopped. "You mean you'd let me wear them? If I could—I mean, I'm bigger than you are, so this is really hypothetical. But if I could?"

Impulsively, Jessie offered, "Sure, why not?"

Cass lowered her head. When she raised it, Jessie saw that her eyes were wet.

"Thanks, Jess."

When Joe arrived, Jessie opened the door for him. He was like a member of the family. Even before he started dating Cass, they had known each other through church. In fact, the two families had been friends for years.

Dad had come in less than fifteen minutes before Joe. Mom was resting. Her father greeted the young man with a firm handshake. Joe was a good basketball player. He played center. Joe already had scholarship offers from colleges that wanted him to play for them, but Jessie knew that he wanted a degree in mechanical engineering so he could join his father's firm.

When Cass entered, the warmth in Joe's eyes lit the room. Jessie wondered if anyone would ever look at her like that.

No way. Sylvia Duncan crooks her little finger and Jamar melts. Not that I like him. It's the principle of the thing. If I looked like Sylvia or Cass or even that crazy Addie Mae, then . . .

After the couple left, Jessie paced the bedroom floor, seeing her reflection in the mirror. *Brown hair. Brown eyes. Brown skin. Too much brown. I want to look special, different.* Jess bit her bottom lip.

An image grew in her mind. *What if . . .* she wondered as she headed for the bathroom. Searching through the shelves beneath the towel rack, Jessie saw the box. Quickly, she stuck her head out the bathroom door.

"Dad! I'm going to take a long bath. Then I'm going to bed," she yelled upstairs.

"Fine," he replied.

The directions on the box were as simple as one, two, three, four. When Jessie finished, she realized that she didn't have a watch. *No big deal. I can estimate the time.*

Jessie sat on a stool. Before she knew it, she was nodding off. Hard knocks on the door woke her.

"Jessie, open this door. You've been in there over an hour," said her father. "Jessie, are you all right?"

"I'm fine, Dad. I just forgot the time," she answered, scampering to the mirror. Snatching up the piece of paper, Jessie reread the instructions. The time limit was twenty minutes! Breathless, Jessie rinsed out her hair. She prayed that since Mom's hair dye was old, an extra fifty minutes wouldn't matter.

"Jessie!"

"Dad, I have to dry off! Then I'll be out. I fell asleep in the tub," she hollered, working fast.

She shampooed her hair five times. But whenever she dared a peek in the mirror, red, red, red hair mocked her. So much red. Frantic, she reread the instructions. *Unless I dye it brown, I have to wait until it grows out. My hair is redder than Julie's and I'm sure not Irish.*

"Jessie, let me in," ordered her mother now.

First, Jess grabbed a towel and wrapped it around her head. Then she dumped cleanser in the sink and scrubbed out the red stains. Two tosses later the bottle of dye and gloves were hidden under an empty Kleenex box in the trash basket. With a twist she unlocked the door.

"What are you up to, young lady?" Mrs. Williams sniffed the air.

"Nothing, Mom. I'm absolutely exhausted. I have to get some sleep." Jessie yawned and skirted around her, speaking fast and moving faster.

"Where are you going? What is that strange smell? Why are you wearing that towel? What's that red splotch on the floor there? I had this gnawing premonition that you were going to do something outrageous. Remove that towel, now." Mom stood with both hands on her hips, a bad sign.

Trapped, Jessie obeyed.

For several seconds her mother simply stared. Wordless, she fled the bathroom. She returned with her husband.

"Jessie, what in the world have you done to yourself? Is this for some new acting part? You've gone too far this time," he said, his voice getting louder with every word. "Honey, can you fix this?"

"I don't think so. Adding more color right away might make Jessie's hair break off. She'll have to wear this for a while."

Jessie darted between her parents, dragging the red-stained towel behind her. Crying, she shut the bedroom door and wrapped the towel around her head. Jessie dived into bed. Her mother followed.

Gently, her mother gathered Jess up in her arms and rocked her. "Oh, Jess."

"It's so hard, Mom. So hard. I wanted to look pretty. That's why I did it," wailed Jessie. "What am I going to do? I can't go to school like this! I can't, Mom. What am I going to do?"

"Honey, I'll call my beautician, but I'm sure she's going to advise that we let it grow out. The hair color you used is very strong and very old. We'll figure something out," soothed Mrs. Williams. "Your hair grows so fast. You'll only be a redhead for a few months. You'll just look . . . dramatic."

"You mean ugly! Oh, Mom! This is the worst thing I ever did!" Jessie thought of Addie Mae, Sylvia, Mr. Reynolds, the audition next week, and Jamar. "I can't let anybody see me, Mom. I look like a joke! I'll be ruined! I hate OPA. I wish I was going to a regular school with my old friends."

"Number one—you could never be ugly. You're my daughter. Number two—this isn't permanent. And number three, you're worn out from your first week. Jess, please, it's not the end of the world."

"Yes, it is, Mom," Jessie sobbed. "Yes, it is."

chapter 4

Later that night, Jessie crept down the hallway. Everyone was asleep. Her Oakland As baseball cap con-
cealed most of the disaster. She pushed Mamatoo's
buzzer—long, short, short, short. All night she had listened for the sound of a sputtering car engine.

"Jess. It is almost one o'clock in the morning! Why
aren't you in bed?" said her grandmother.

"I have to talk to you."

"Why are you wearing a baseball cap?"

With one fling, the hat sailed across the room and
landed on the floor. Jess waited for Mamatoo's reaction. There was none. Her grandmother went to the
kitchen, put on the teakettle, hung her coat up, went
into her bedroom, and emerged ten minutes later in a
scarlet Chinese robe with a slinky dragon embroidered
on the back. Not a word said.

"Did you bring down a copy of the play you'll be auditioning for?" she asked, getting out a packet of herbal teas.

"Mamatoo, look at my hair!"

"It's still there. I am thankful for that. At least you didn't hack it off. I saw it. Thank heavens you have that gorgeous brown skin. With that shade of red, you need it. I wouldn't get it braided or use heat on it, Jess." She handed Jessie a mug.

"Mamatoo, what are you talking about? I look terrible!"

Proceeding as if Jessie had not spoken, Mamatoo glanced up. "I've got some powerful conditioner in my bathroom. Tomorrow, I mean later on today, I'll give you some. Then we'll rinse it out, roll your hair on curlers, and let it dry." She sipped her rose hip tea. "The copy of the play?"

"I'll bring one down in the morning. First thing. And then we can do my hair?" Jessie asked.

"Nine A.M. sharp. Finish that tea and go to bed, child. No more hysterics. If you've got the stuff of a real actress, you can go to school and pull this snafu off," she said.

"That won't be easy. I am a walking fire engine."

Her grandmother laughed. It was a full, husky sound. "Just tell the truth. You were trying out a different look, right? So, say that. Honestly, Jess, once you get used to the color—" Giggling, she set her mug down.

Outraged, Jessie stared. She couldn't believe that Mamatoo was laughing at her.

"All right, I'm under control now. I am absolutely relieved you didn't go blond. In your case, it definitely wouldn't have been more fun!" With that she bent over in laughter.

The sound was infectious. *Mamatoo is right. It could be worse. But not by much.*

By Sunday evening, Jessie knew she was stuck with red hair for a while. Cass hadn't even teased her. She arranged her sister's hair in an attractive style and lent her barrettes to wear. When Cass suggested outfits that wouldn't clash too much, Jessie paid close attention. Like déjà vu, she found herself trying on outfit after outfit.

"Thanks for helping me, Cassandra."

Cass folded a pale yellow sweater. "You're my sister. My pretty sister, even with red hair."

Jessie squirmed out of the blue jeans dress. "How can I feel good about Dad calling me his 'brown bird' and you his 'golden bird'?"

"You can't. But that's Dad's problem. I don't think he means to hurt you, Jess. I'm light skinned. You're brown skinned. My eyes are lighter than yours and my hair is straighter. That just means that the white in our family came out more in me. What's so great about knowing that I'm light *not* because there was intermarriage in our family history, but because there was slavery and the abuse of our women! Think about what that means for me, Jess!"

Cass's harsh words shocked Jess. Her sister paced

the floor. *What is going on with Cass? She acts ashamed of her color and all, not proud.*

"I've got too much pressure to deal with right now. Joe and I had an argument—a bad one. He wants us to go to the same college. How can I promise that?" Cass started to cry, but she held her hand up to keep her sister away. "I made the squad, but I decided not to run for captain this year. Too much is going on and coming home and dealing with you hating me is driving me up a wall."

"I don't hate you, Cass. I just wish—"

"That you looked like me. Well, think about that, Jess. I don't feel ashamed. But looking like this is nothing to flaunt." Her sister blew her nose.

"Cass, I'm sorry about you and Joe. I love you. And I won't read your diary anymore. It wasn't boring."

Her sister faced her. "Truce, Jess?"

For the first time, Jessie saw past her sister's appearance. What she saw was a big sister who was very upset and who loved her. Too many people, black *and* white, did not feel like Cass. They believed that the whiter you looked, the prettier you were. Jessie knew this. All too well. The secret hurt ached. *Even grown-ups who are supposed to see children for themselves, not their color, don't. But my sister is different. And better!*

"Truce, Cass."

On the way to school Monday, Jessie scrutinized her reflection in the car mirror. Rolled back, tucked in, and parted on the side, the style that Cass had created minimized the shock of the color.

During Family Hour, her classmates gaped, but one glare from Jessie cut off any comments. Mr. Reynolds's eyebrows lifted, but he said nothing. The other Fours stared. He called the roll. He got to Addie Mae Cooper. The class waited.

"Addie Mae Cooper."

The teacher raised his head. His eyes settled on her. She pursed her lips and stared back at him. Finally, he shrugged his shoulders.

"Obidie Cooper?"

"Here."

The disappointment in his face showed. Jessie wanted to reach over and shake some sense into Obidie. What was the big deal about the name Addie Mae Collins anyway?

When they moved to their groups, Jessie spoke up.

"Obidie, who is Addie Mae Collins?"

Clad in a "Free South Africa" black, green, and red T-shirt, and wearing a "Stop Apartheid" button, Obidie was a walking protest movement.

"Why do you keep bothering me with that?"

Jessie countered, "Why do you keep it a secret?"

"If my hair looked like a fire hydrant, I'd mind my own business. If you were up on your African-American history, you wouldn't have to ask. Stay out of my business," said Obidie, "and I'll stay out of yours, Jessie."

Jessie started to say something, but stopped. The best thing to do was to ask the one person who would know and would tell her—Dad.

Maria sighed. "We don't have time for this. I have a suggestion for our community project. Julie thinks it is a good idea."

Julie nodded.

Obidie frowned. "What is it?"

"There is a home for senior citizens in the neighborhood. My mother volunteers there. She says that it's a nice place, but the old people don't get enough company." Maria took a breath. "So why don't we go there and put on a program for them?"

Jessie spoke up. "What kind of program? We have auditions to get ready for plus homework."

"And nothing can get in the way of my getting selected for the African Dance Troupe!"

"This wouldn't stop you," said Julie.

Maria frowned. "What's the problem? All we have to do is to present what we know. They have a piano so I can play something. Come on, we can present our audition pieces."

"That sounds disconnected. We need a story to hold it together," Jessie said, getting into it. "We need a hook—something that connects us. This could work." Her mind tumbled. Suddenly, she knew what they needed to do!

Jessie spoke up. "Why not do our own version of the musical *Dreamgirls?* My grandmother took me to see it years ago. Why not a short play? I could narrate. A play about four girls with dreams."

"My mother could videotape it," Maria said.

"And we can share the videotape with the class," added Obidie.

"But Mr. Reynolds said we have to plan this carefully. That's part of our grade." Jessie frowned. "We need to do more."

"Why not meet at my house after school this week? We could meet every week at somebody's house. That would make us look good to Mr. Reynolds," Maria said. "My father can drive everybody home."

The group agreed on Wednesday as their first meeting date. That way they could present an outline of their project to the class on Friday.

Jessie managed to survive the rest of the day. Going to OPA made looking strange easier. Creative kids were expected to be eccentric. *And I sure qualify,* she thought.

When Jess entered the theater, she searched for an empty seat in the rear. Jamar was in the back, not up front with Sylvia. He smiled and beckoned to the seat next to his. Biting her lip, Jessie mumbled a greeting.

"You changed your hair," he said.

Jessie stared into sparkling eyes. She wanted to say something smart and snappy. Nothing came out.

Jamar filled the silent gap. "I like it. Are you ready for the auditions this week?"

"No. I'll just watch and learn." She peered around

to see if anybody noticed Jamar talking to her. All of this was new and very unsettling.

"That's not your style. You're too much like my cousin, Sylvia. Only center stage for you," said Jamar.

"Your cousin? Sylvia Duncan is your cousin?" sputtered Jessie.

"Yeah. She likes to act like a big sister, especially since I came from another school," he said.

"Why did you leave your old school?"

"Drugs and guns. My folks don't want me to become another drive-by statistic." His face hardened. "My brother was shot last spring. For being in the wrong place at the wrong time. So we moved."

Jessie listened in horror. "Is he OK?"

"Not really. He has nightmares. So my parents put his bed in my room. He feels safer there. I saw him get shot. He's only six." Jamar stared at his hands. "I couldn't get to him in time. Some kids in a car started shooting. Reggie was playing on the sidewalk. The bullet hit him in the arm. Blood was everywhere. They never found out who did it."

"I'm so sorry, Jamar. Is your brother's arm healed?"

Jamar sighed. "Yeah. Reggie has no problems using his arm. But I don't think he'll ever be the same happy, free kid brother I used to have. I'm going to make sure this shooting and killing stops!"

"So that's why you want to become a United States senator. Your goal is to use your power to change that," said Jessie.

"You remember?" He smiled. "Yeah. Change that and a lot of other bad things. Acting classes will help me become a better communicator. Brains, determination, and persuasive skills are important to have. I'm going to make life better for black people."

Jessie wanted to say that in her opinion his communication skills were already outstanding. But she shut her mouth.

Mr. Reynolds and Miss Baker gathered the class together. The new acting exercise required concentration. It was like a game. One person went up on stage and mimed a person, thing, or action. The others guessed what the person was doing. When the guess was correct, Miss Baker shouted, "Freeze!" The actor onstage froze into place.

"Freeze!" meant that you had used your mind and body so well that others could figure out what you were doing. Every student wanted to hear that word. After Miss Baker yelled the magic word, another student assumed the frozen position and started a new mime that flowed out of the previous one. It was like making a silent movie, but more fun and work.

After several wrong guesses from the audience, each student had to tell the class what he or she had been attempting to mime. Then the student sat down and the exercise continued with someone new. Both Jessie and Jamar were good enough to hear Miss Baker say, "Freeze!" After class, they walked out together. Jessie ducked her head when River winked at her.

That night Jessie rehearsed with Mamatoo. She'd

selected Manyara, the rude sister in the African folk-tale version of Cinderella. Jess couldn't quite feel this character. Reading Manyara's part felt like trying on tight shoes.

"Jess, are you going after a big part or a strong part?" asked Mamatoo.

"A big part."

"Then you have a serious problem. Manyara does not work for you and you know it. But there is a character that will."

Jessie thought.

"Focus on your strengths. Come on. What did you do for your audition?" demanded Mamatoo.

"Sojourner Truth. Oh, how can I be so dense! The old woman who foretells what Manyara will encounter," Jessie exclaimed. "It's a small part, but a good one."

"Now we can rehearse." Her grandmother smiled.

By the end of the evening, Jessie felt much more assured. She was scheduled to try out on Friday after school. Tuesday faded into Wednesday. After school she joined Maria, Julie, and Obidie. They walked three blocks to Maria's house.

It stood out. The one-story pink stucco home was surrounded by houses on each side. Gorgeous, brilliant flowers and expertly sculpted bushes and trees framed the home. An elaborate black wrought-iron fence bordered the yard. Jessie thought it was beautiful.

Jessie had never been in the home of a Mexican-American family before. The living room was spacious.

In one corner was a grand piano. Potted plants flourished in the afternoon sun. Art hung on the walls. Books were everywhere. But what caught her attention was the beautiful photographs of family members that hung on the walls or sat on top of the piano and anywhere else there was room.

Jessie saw Maria and her parents with two older boys. *They must be Maria's brothers,* Jessie thought. In some of the framed photographs, she saw a lovely little girl with Maria. Jessie wondered who she was.

Maria was fortunate. Jessie had read that people who had lost their belongings in the fire suffered more if they had been unable to save family albums, videos, and photographs. If the fire had touched this house . . .

Mrs. Hernandez, a slender woman, welcomed them. For an hour and a half the girls talked and organized. They passed the notepad from one to the other, taking turns. The punch and sandwiches were delicious.

"I think we have a plan," said Maria.

Obidie added, "And that means a good grade."

"This is beginning to get interesting," said Jessie.

Julie spoke up. "I like this."

"Wait until you meet these people. They are so appreciative, and what you're doing will bring so much happiness." Mrs. Hernandez stood by the piano. "Maria, won't you play something for your friends?"

"Oh, Mama, they don't want to hear me."

All three girls yelled, "Yes, we do!"

Maria got up. In seconds, she became a different

person. Her hands touched the keys and beautiful music filled the room. Maria seemed unaware of them. Jessie knew how she felt. *Just like I do when I really get into acting.* The last note lingered. Jessie led the applause.

Blushing, Maria curtsied. "That was the theme from the *New World Symphony* by Dvořák."

Julie smiled. "You are better than anyone in my performance class. Maybe we could do something together for the project—a piano and violin piece."

"Sure. We've got a lot to chose from."

Julie nodded.

"My daughter Maria practices three hours every day," said her mother.

The girls were shocked.

Shoot! I thought I worked hard! Maria doesn't boast about her gift. She doesn't need to, thought Jessie, wondering if Addie Mae was thinking the same thing. There were no clues on her face.

Maria explained. "My *compadres*, my godparents, got me interested in music when I was a little girl. One time when we went to Mexico to see the rest of our family, they took me to a concert. When I heard the pianist, I wanted to do what she did."

At that moment, two cats, both Siamese, strolled into the living room. One rubbed against Maria's leg and purred. Without warning, Julie jumped up. She threw on her jacket and hoisted her book bag. Tears glittered in her eyelashes.

"I have to go! Thanks." Out of the house she ran.

"Julie! Wait. My husband will drive you home," yelled Maria's mother. But the girl was gone.

"Maria, what is going on with Julie?" Jessie asked.

"All I know is that Julie lives a few blocks over. Her family moved here around December. We walk to school together. I've never been to her house. She doesn't talk much."

"Did she tell you why her family moved?" asked Obidie.

Maria shook her head. "No, and I won't ask."

The front door opened. Mr. Hernandez came in. He hugged Maria, then his wife. The two of them went into the kitchen, laughing and talking.

"Excuse them. My parents are very close. Our whole family is. They've been married for twenty years."

"You've got it made, Maria," Obidie said in a low, sad voice. Then she asked where the bathroom was.

Later as they left, Jessie noticed a white van that had "Hernandez Landscaping and Gardening" painted on the side. That explained the lush foliage.

There was plenty of room in the Hernandezes' beige station wagon. Obidie lived about fifteen minutes away. A woman was waiting in front of the apartment building.

"That's my mother. My father is still at the fire station. If he was home, he'd be standing out here waiting for me. He hates for Mama to get cold or be out here alone. He says that it is too dangerous. He really looks after us. Thanks for the ride, Mr. Hernandez." She jumped out of the car.

"Nobody asked her about her father. Why would she say all that?" asked Jessie. She and Maria threw up their hands.

During Family Hour on Thursday, they firmed up the draft of their project. Maria was unanimously chosen to share their idea with the class. They brainstormed a list of what was needed to do the project. It took minutes to divide the work.

Jessie made it through the rest of the day. Afterward, at home, she practiced the part of the Old Woman. Friday would be a big day. After a quick shower, she went upstairs. Her parents were huddled together in the study reviewing the finances of the bookstore.

"I may not have to worry about going away to school," Cass said. "If the store goes under, what will we do?"

Jessie shook her head.

It was impossible to fall asleep. Jess knew that Maria, Julie, and Obidie were facing the same Friday she was—classes all day and auditions in the afternoon. Obidie had been as tight as a knot. Even Maria acted antsy. It was strange to see that only Julie seemed oblivious to the tension. Figuring Julie out was not easy.

On Friday morning, Jessie sailed into Home Base wearing her lucky T-shirt and old blue jeans. Maria strolled into Family Hour humming and moving her hands like she was playing the piano. Obidie glided majestically in. Only Julie acted like a normal person.

Their group presented last. Maria outlined their plan with precision and flair. The class applauded.

"I am very proud of you. Now the hard work starts. I want a report on your project every Friday. What diversity! Working on the upcoming election, holding a food drive for the homeless, planting trees with the Park Service—I am impressed." Mr. Reynolds grinned. "Now go out there and make it a good day."

The Fours sighed in unison.

Lunch was quiet. Audition fever ran high. Somehow they had taken to eating together every day after their first day. Good Lucks were exchanged around the table. After school ended, Jessie rushed to her locker to get her copy of the script. She stopped in the bathroom. Her hair was still red. It might even be redder. It sure looked that way. Jessie took a deep breath and ran to the theater.

There weren't many students inside. River was there.

"I'm not auditioning. Miss Baker wants me to help her get the flyers out for the major performances." River smiled.

"What major performances? What are you talking about?"

"What's going on here is for practice, not performance. You'll go through four or five of these every semester. But there are two big events. That's where performing comes in," explained River.

"What are they?"

"Right before the holidays in December, we have a series of productions in music, art, theater, and dance. That's what your family comes to and anyone else. But in May we hold the big yearly fund-raiser. Important people come to that one, real stars, and the audience buys tickets." River stood up. "Miss Baker wants me. Break a leg. Oh, Jamar read the part of the king. I think he'll get it."

Now Jessie understood why mostly sixth graders were auditioning. These auditions were small fish to fry for the older students. They had done this kind of work before. *Well, it's still big stuff to me,* Jessie thought. *Mamatoo says that practicing your craft is important.* When her name was called, she sat on the stool downstage center, placed the script on the black stand, and indicated that she was ready.

Reader's theater was tough work. She had to read the part of the old woman and use her voice and gestures to make her character believable. Sylvia read the part of the narrator and cued Jessie in.

Onstage focus! That's what Mamatoo said. In the voice of an old woman, she read the part.

Jess left hoping that the list posted on Monday morning would have her name on it.

I wonder how Obidie, Julie, and Maria did. We forgot to share our phone numbers!

The weekend limped along like a sick cat. Nobody had much to say. Mamatoo was in bed with a cold. There was no Friday or Saturday night date for Cass.

On Sunday Jessie and Cass went to the movies. They hadn't done this for a long time. It turned out to be fun.

By the time Monday morning arrived, Jessie's nails were bitten almost to the quick. Her first stop was the small theater. The list was posted. Jessie saw Jamar's name by *King*. She scanned farther down. Her part wasn't big, but it was all hers.

"Old woman—Jessie Williams! I did it! I got the part I went after!"

"You sure <u>did</u>!" said a familiar voice behind her.

"Jamar, you're the king!" said Jessie. "We perform next Monday and Tuesday."

They grinned at each other and went off to their separate classes. Today Jessie was eager to get to Family Hour.

"I got the part of the old woman! What about you all?"

"I get to play in one of the lunch-bag recitals. So does Julie. I can't believe that I have to be ready in one week. They really push you at this school," Maria said. "What about you, Obidie?"

Obidie was silent. The group waited.

"My name isn't Obidie anymore." Her eyes welled with tears. "My name is Mkiwa, mm-*KEE*-wah. It's Kiswahili."

"What does this name mean?" Jessie asked.

Addie Mae bit her lip. "Orphaned child."

"Come on! You're no orphan. You've got a father and a mother!" Maria admonished.

"Maria, you'd never understand," said Addie Mae, her face closed. "I did get a place in the African Dance Troupe." There was no elation in her voice.

Quietly but not unsympathetically, Julie handed Addie Mae a Kleenex. Mr. Reynolds started the morning ritual.

"Cooper, Obidie?"

"That's not my name anymore. You can call me whatever you want to," she mumbled.

"OK." Mr. Reynolds paused, calm and in control as ever. "Let's just go with Cooper for now. Fair?"

Addie Mae nodded.

Twenty minutes later, the four girls had exchanged phone numbers and decided to meet at Jessie's house on Wednesday, then Addie Mae/Mkiwa's, and finally Julie's. Mr. Reynolds passed out a schedule listing the schoolwide events for the rest of the semester. Parent volunteers were needed. A slip was attached for parents to check and sign.

Every parent was required to volunteer at least once a semester. This was one of the conditions for admission to the Oakland Performing Arts Middle School. Jessie stuck it in her book bag. She had reports to give and two essay tests ahead of her. Another long day.

Winter Festival events were announced in her last class. The festival would begin on Monday, December 14, and conclude with a holiday arts and crafts fair on Saturday, December 19. There would be events each night—a talent show, dance recitals, concerts, and more. The play was scheduled for Friday, December 18. Jessie clapped when she heard the title. It was by Mr. Reynolds! He had taken the story of Harriet Tubman and created a play!

Mamatoo had directed that play two years ago for a youth theater in Los Angeles. Jessie knew it inside out and backward. She had never made the connection between Mr. Reynolds her teacher, and Mr. Reynolds the playwright.

Later that afternoon as Jessie headed for her locker, she noticed large posters in the hallways. She stopped in front of one. "Back-to-School Dance, Friday, September 25th, 7:30–9:30."

"Oh, no! Not that dance. I don't have the energy for a back-to-school dance. Just getting to OPA and home and back again with my homework done is killing me! I don't need any extracurricular activities to round out my life!" Jessie muttered to herself.

The Student Council would be selling refreshments. Groups from the school would provide live and recorded music. Everyone was supposed to attend, especially sixth graders. Jessie's stomach plummeted.

A real dance with boys. I'll have to figure out some way to get out of going. The very thought of walking into that huge lunchroom/auditorium with her red hair was unthinkable.

Jessie sighed. *It's too much. If this is what growing up is about, I don't like it. No wonder Cass is having a hard time. Just when I get over one scary thing, another one pops up. When will it stop?*

chapter 5

On Wednesday afternoon, the Fours concluded their meeting. Plans for the performance at the senior citizen home were progressing. Mom handed Jessie a stack of jackets. "Come on, I'll drive everyone home just as we arranged."

Chattering, the girls piled into the station wagon. Julie was the last one to get in. She sat next to Jessie, up front.

"It sure looks bare up here," she said. "I haven't been up here in a while. I mean I saw the hills before the fire. But I didn't know the fire burned so much."

"Me neither," Maria chimed in. "You were lucky, Jessie. The fire stopped just feet away from your house."

"Now that would have scared me," Mkiwa added.

"Think about the people whose homes burned

down. Imagine returning and finding only ashes, a chimney, and burned pieces of your life," murmured Jessie.

Mkiwa shook her head. "I can't."

Julie spoke up. "Good. You don't want to know. None of you do. It's horrible."

Jessie turned toward her. "How do you know, Julie?"

"A lot of my friends got burned out. My best friend did." Her voice was barely a whisper, but the words carried to the back of the station wagon. The remainder of the drive was quiet.

After dropping everyone off, Mom started the drive back to their own house. Jessie thought about the afternoon. The group had accomplished a great deal during the community project meeting. A date for visiting the Evergreen Residential Manor had been set. Maria's suggestion to present their audition pieces was voted in. Using a *Dreamgirls* format, Jessie had written the presentation story line.

Each of them would share her dream through her performance. Jessie would narrate the story of four girls who succeeded in getting admitted to the Oakland Performing Arts Middle School. As each girl took her place, Jessie would introduce them. She would go last with her Sojourner Truth speech. At the end, they would bow.

"Jessie, is there a special event you'd like your dad and me to volunteer for? What time do you want to

leave for the dance on Friday? Aren't you excited?"
Mrs. Williams smiled. "Aren't you lucky to have such
nice friends? But I am concerned about Julie and—
what is her name—Mkiwa? Don't they seem troubled
to you? Especially Julie. Being in our house was very
uncomfortable for her. I don't know why, do you?"

"No, Mom. But as soon as the bus headed up
Woodglen Road, she got shaky. During the last four
blocks, she stared out the window like she was searching for something. Then Julie couldn't wait to leave
our house. Then she was the last one to get in the car. I
don't know what's going on," said Jessie. "She's
strange. I can't figure her out."

"Well. Now, I don't want you worried about anything and that includes the bookstore. This is your
time to blossom like a budding rose."

Jessie focused on where she and her mother were.
Almost home. The narrow, winding road up the hill to
their house stretched before her. It was restful inside
the car. The sunset softened some of the grim landscape.

"Jessie, did you hear what I asked you?" Mrs. Williams braked for a stop sign.

"You and Dad decide. I'm not going to the dance on
Friday. Cass and I can't help being worried about the
bookstore. We don't want Dad to have to sell it. And
Mom, face the facts, I am more of a bright red cactus
than a budding rose."

"There are flowering cacti, Jess. Though you are a

prickly one lately. As for the business, your dad and I have some ideas. Now, young lady, you will be going to the dance. Cass can drive you and pick you up."

Too weary to protest, Jessie settled for silence. *I wonder if our parents have been plotting together. Nobody in the group wants to go to the dance.*

Family Hour was unusually subdued on Friday. The two rehearsals for *Mufaro's Beautiful Daughters* had gone well. But Jessie welcomed the opportunity to practice once more before the performance. The auditions for *Harriet Tubman* would be held in two weeks.

Mr. Reynolds had emphasized that working behind the scenes was just as valuable as acting out front. Jessie had heard that speech countless times before. Building sets, props, making costumes, working on make-up, lighting, sound, and publicity were critical to the success of a play. But for Jess it was a good part or nothing.

Julie rubbed her forehead. "Is everybody going to the dance tonight?"

They nodded.

"I told my mother I'm not going to dress up. I didn't come here to go to parties and stand around looking silly." Mkiwa's mouth said one thing, but she looked nervous.

"Cooper, you're the dancer in the group," Jessie said. "Of the four of us, I figured you'd be excited."

Mkiwa snapped, "Well, I'm not. Dancing for an audience is not the same as dancing with some boy."

"And having the seventh and eighth graders there makes it worse. Sometimes I feel like I'm wearing a badge that says, 'Sixth grader, starting from scratch.'" Julie pursed her lips.

Maria snorted. "Take all that and add having your folks standing guard over you."

Jessie sighed. "Julie and Maria, can you dance?"

They nodded.

"Well, I can't and I don't have time to learn."

Julie smiled. "Just act like you can. Move to the music. If I can, you can."

"What! Did you make a joke, girl?" Mkiwa asked.

Standing straighter, Julie turned to face Mkiwa. "I guess I did. Right now, we need a laugh."

But Jessie wasn't in a happy mood. "Right now, I'm the laugh—a laughing mess."

"I tried to convince my parents that volunteering for something else would be better. That was a waste of breath. Knowing my father, they'll show up for every dance. At least I convinced my brothers to stay home," said Maria.

Julie let out a breath. "The good thing is that we won't be alone! At least we'll have each other."

Later with script in hand, Jessie took her place behind the stage curtains. It was time for *Mufaro's Beautiful Daughters*—the final rehearsal, full dress and strictly business. The theater darkened. The curtains rose. Seven stools stood in a row behind seven stands. On each stool was a long scarf made from African *kente* cloth. The lighting technician clicked on the top lighting. In single file, the actors walked out.

Dressed in white T-shirts and black slacks, the actors opened their scripts and placed them on the stands. In unison they draped the striped green, red, black, yellow, and orange panels from the stools over their left shoulders and took their seats. Heads bowed, they waited.

As narrator, Sylvia sat on the first stool. Jamar was at the other end. In the background, a student turned on the sound effects tape. Sylvia's clear voice started the story, "A long time ago, in a certain place in Africa . . ." Jessie shivered.

Twenty minutes passed before Sylvia uttered the words, "The End." Jamar gave Jessie a thumbs-up sign!

Miss Baker and Mr. Reynolds clapped.

"Now, that's what we want on Monday and Tuesday. Remember this is a reading. Use your voice to make your character distinctive," said Miss Baker.

Mr. Reynolds added, "Respect the author's language. Don't throw away a single word. See you Monday at lunch period. One more thing—tonight is our first schoolwide event for the year, the dance. So show up!"

"Will you be at the dance, Jessie?" Jamar asked as they walked out.

Jessie frowned. "Yeah. I have to go."

"You mean you don't want to go? What's wrong?"

Part of Jessie wanted to crawl under a rock and hide, but Jamar stood there. "Look, Jamar, I can't dance! Now you know."

"Hey, Jess, don't worry about it. You'll do fine. I'm a good teacher. See you there."

Rooted to the floor, Jessie couldn't believe her ears! *Jamar is going to teach me how to dance? I can't handle this.*

Instead of taking the bus home, Jessie caught a bus to the Bay Area Rapid Transit train station. The acronym for the system of trains that ran around the Bay Area and through an underground tunnel beneath the bay waters was BART. Jessie walked onto one of the white train cars and took a seat.

The train left her two blocks from the Williamses' African-American Bookstore. With popular restaurants on both sides, the bookstore had to look good. Painted gray and edged in a glossy black, with two large display windows, the store looked inviting and prosperous.

Jessie spotted her father chatting with a customer. She saw two employees who had worked there for years, John Mitchell and Margaret Green. They were busy unloading books.

"Hi, Jessie! How's school going?" asked Margaret, a retired schoolteacher. "You dyed your hair."

Sometimes Jessie forgot that she was wearing a fire truck on her head. "I'm trying out a new look."

Margaret's expression was skeptical. Jessie caved in.

"OK. What you are staring at is the result of one of

my infamous *What if* experiments. I fell asleep with the hair dye on."

"I see why your father comes in here some mornings pulling his hair out over you." She winked at Jessie.

John smiled. "Jess, you are growing up." John had always been like an uncle to her father. Retired from the army, John enjoyed working for his friend.

Her father beckoned to Margaret to ring up the customer's stack of books. Today, his eyes were clearer. Jessie noticed that the dark circles had faded. Even the burn on his hand didn't stand out as much.

"Now this is a surprise. Why aren't you home? Anything wrong, Jessie?" he asked.

"I didn't want to go home right away, Dad. I need to talk to you. First, Cass and I are worried about the bookstore. Mom said you two had some plans."

"We do. With Margaret's help, I'm going to start doing book fairs in schools and churches, and branch out to different conferences," he said, glancing around to make sure that each customer was being served.

Jessie's shoulders relaxed. "So the store isn't going under?"

"Not if I can help it. What else do you have on your mind?" He wiped his glasses with a handkerchief from his back pocket.

Jessie thought. She wasn't ready to talk about the dance. Or Jamar. "It can wait. You got anything I can do? I don't have much homework, Dad."

"Thanks, Jess. We've got an author coming in to

read tonight from his latest novel. You know how to arrange the display and autograph tables." He tweaked her cheek and went over to a customer.

Since OPA had started, Jessie hadn't been able to work at the bookstore. With auditions, books to read, and more homework than the law allowed, her time was packed. Dad had insisted that she zero in on her schoolwork and forget the store.

But Jessie missed being there two days a week, especially on Saturdays, finding books for customers, using the computer, taking orders, and so much more. Dad had wanted to pay her, but since it was a family store, she didn't think that was fair. Her parents gave her an allowance. That was enough.

She headed for the reading room in the rear of the store. Jess entered another world. Posters, signed and numbered lithographs, sculpture, African clothing, and framed photographs of famous writers who had come to the store graced the walls.

On one, Dad had displayed large photographs of his heroes. Often Jessie wondered if she was being scrutinized by Marcus Garvey, Elijah Muhammad, Malcolm X, Booker T. Washington, Mary McLeod Bethune, David Walker, Fannie Lou Hammer, Dr. King, and the rest of the faces. Solemn as judges, they watched her. Jessie got to work.

When her father came in, he whistled. "You did a fine job. Thank you, daughter. I'll run you home and come back."

Jessie hesitated. Something tugged at the edge of her mind. It had to do with Addie Mae and the way Mr. Reynolds sighed each time he called out one of her African names.

Jessie thought, *What did he say? That Addie Mae was named after someone special. And then Addie Mae told him that she was related to the Collins family in Birmingham, Alabama. When she got mad at me, she told me I should know what her real name meant, if I knew my African-American history. Hmmm . . . Dad would know.*

"Dad, there's this girl in my Home Base group. She keeps changing her real name to African names," said Jessie. "And it makes Mr. Reynolds furious."

"What's her real name?"

"Addie Mae Cooper. But she told Mr. Reynolds that she was a part of the Collins family in Birmingham, Alabama. Who is Addie Mae Collins?"

Dad's expression shifted from curiosity to sorrow. "That name brings back painful memories. Addie Mae Collins. Denise McNair. Carol Robertson. Cynthia Wesley. Four girls. Four schoolchildren." He rubbed his forehead.

"Dad, what's wrong?"

"On September 15, 1963, those four girls were murdered. Some white racist bombed the Sixteenth Street Baptist Church in Birmingham, Alabama, while the girls were attending Sunday school class. They were killed barely two weeks after Dr. King delivered his 'I have a dream' speech," he said.

"Oh, Dad! Why would someone bomb a church? Especially on a Sunday with people there?"

He bit his lip. "Jessie, whoever did it wanted to kill black families. Racism is a sick, destructive force. Those murders were a warning to blacks in Birmingham and all over this country."

"What kind of warning?"

Her father's face froze the same way Jamar's had when he talked about his kid brother, Reggie. "A warning that shouted, 'We'll kill you and your children even in church if you try to vote, eat in our restaurants, use our drinking fountains and bathrooms, live, work, go to school with the same freedom that we have. Stay in your place or die.' And Addie Mae Collins had the sweetest face."

"What a horrible thing to do! So Addie Mae was named after one of the girls. They are relatives. Imagine having to carry that history around."

"It's a heavy load. When those children were murdered, this country erupted. That was one of the tragedies that fueled the civil rights movement in the 1960s."

"Dad, do you have books about that?"

"Of course. I'll go through the shelves and bring some home. Why this sudden interest?" he asked.

Jessie thought about Jamar and life in their old neighborhood. Her eyes swept the room. The heroes gazed down at her. "That could have been me or Cass if we'd been born then. I want to know more."

"Excellent. I want you to learn as much as possible about your history."

They left in the van. Dad needed the van to haul books and display stands around. Going to the store had been a good idea. She'd have to do it more often. Too much was new in her life: classes, the upcoming reader's theater performance, auditions for the big play, her group project, and the dance tonight!

"Dad, why do I have to go to the dance tonight?" she asked.

He shifted gears. "Because your mother said so."

"Seriously, Dad."

"Do you remember how you used to mope around when your sister went to a dance or party? I do. Now it's your turn. I've noticed your efforts at school. I'm impressed with your determination," said her father. "You deserve some fun, Jessie."

Jessie sighed inwardly. Her dad thought he was doing her a favor!

When Jess got home, Cass was on the telephone. She dropped her books and opened the doors to the deck. Before the fire, lounging on the deck and reading or acting to the towering trees had been great. Now the trees were gone. Now, when Jessie spoke, her voice sounded lonely. Laughter came from the living room. Cass.

I hope she's talking to Joe. They belong together like Mom and Dad.

That made her think about Jamar. They talked

every day. Jessie cringed at the thought of Jamar seeing his little brother get shot in the arm. The fact that no one had been charged or arrested didn't shock her. Before they'd moved to this house, her family had lived in a neighborhood that a crack house had ruined, street by street.

But life in the old neighborhood hadn't always been dangerous and deadly. Jessie could visualize their small wooden house on a normal tree-lined street in the Oakland flatlands in a predominantly African-American community. The neighborhood school had been less than three blocks away.

Jess recalled the good memories of going to sleep and waking up to the sounds of African-American music, talk, and life. So many happy times playing with friends. Then a crack dealer moved into a house across the street from her family.

Before long, Dad had made her and Cass stay inside and away from the front door and the windows. No more playing outside. Then he had black iron bars installed on the windows of the house and iron screen doors. Strange cars sped up and down their street at all hours of the night. People came in and out of that house twenty-four hours a day. Fights and loud arguments started. Neighbors who could move, did.

None of her parents' telephone calls or letters to the police stopped the crack dealer or his customers. Dad's attempts to organize a block resistance group failed, after several of the neighbors received threats from the gang that worked with the man in the house across the street. After a shooting one Saturday night that left a man dead, Dad started searching for a safer home for them.

Even though she understood why her parents had used the inheritance money to buy the house in the hills, their decision had seriously altered her life. Jessie stared around her. Living up here in the hills wasn't so wonderful. They had to drive to get to anything, even the newspaper. The people who lived in the hills were mostly white. Her parents were polite, but they tried to maintain their ties to the church and community they had left in the flatlands.

She had lost friends from the old neighborhood. Jess missed Jackie, Cherise, and Derrick. They had been pals since kindergarten. Seeing them in church some Sundays was not enough.

There's no real neighborhood up here, just a bunch of houses. I wonder where Jamar lives. Shoot, I'll see him at the dance. It's only a few hours away. Jess leaned against the railing. She felt her sister come close.

"You know what you're going to wear?" asked Cass. "Joe and I will take you. Tell me what time you want us to pick you up."

"You and Joe made up?"

Cass threw up her arms and danced around the deck. "He told me that he loves me and no matter where we go to college, we'll be together. And, something else. I'll tell you if you swear not to tell Dad or Mom. You promise?"

"Sure, sure. What?"

"We're getting engaged right after we graduate from Oakland High next June. Joe's saving to buy me an engagement ring," Cass whispered. "With a real diamond."

"What, Cass? Dad and Mom will kill you! There's no way they'll go for that. How can you go to college and study to be a doctor and get married?"

"We won't get married until after we graduate from college. Joe and I have it all planned. We won't have children until I've completed my medical residency."

Jessie gulped air. Her mind raced like an Indy 500 car engine. What in the world was wrong with Cass? Getting married and even thinking about having any kids was a million years away! What about years of college and those extra years for med school? *Is my sister going crazy? Marriage. Kids. Those are words that don't belong in either of our mouths.*

"Kids! What do you mean, babies? Babies means sex. I wouldn't even think those words around Dad or Mom. And I don't want to know what you and Joe do privately. I'm too young to handle this." She threw up her hands. "How can you and Joe think about this grown-up stuff? You don't even have jobs!"

"We know all that."

Her sister's answer was confusing. How close were Cass and Joe? No. Any of those ideas were out of the question. Cass never took risks. She always thought everything out to the nth degree before doing anything, even selecting a shade of lipstick. Cass lived for goals, setting and achieving them. Nothing got in her way.

Part of Jessie flared in resentment at the sight of her sister twirling around the deck. Cassandra always got to experience the important events in life first. Cassandra made teenager first; got to drive a car, have a boyfriend, be a cheerleader; and now, get engaged.

When my turn comes around, it's already happened in the family.

"Jess, you'll keep my secret, won't you?"

But Jessie's thoughts whirled like a tornado. Now Cass was making plans with Joe to get engaged and eventually marry and have a family. That just did not sound like Cass. Was her do-right-all-the-time, goody-girl sister changing? Jessie looked at Cass. There was intense joy and determination sparkling in her eyes.

"Cass, what's wrong with you?"

Her sister stopped dancing. "Nothing. I'm in love. Joe and I are back together. Nothing matters more than that."

"School does. True, Cass?"

"Oh, Jess, you can't comprehend how I feel. But one day you will. When you fall in love, your whole world changes. I thought I'd die if I lost Joe. We're closer than ever. Now, let's get you ready for your first big dance. No more talk about me."

Jessie protested. "I can get myself ready. All I have to do is to take a shower, brush the burning bush on top of my head, and throw on my lucky clothes."

"Would you try a couple of things on? You don't

have to wear them. Just let me be a big sister, please," asked Cass.

"I want to do this my way." Jessie's voice wavered.

To her surprise, the response was, "Have it your way." Cass actually shrugged her shoulders and headed back into the house.

"Wait a minute. Don't just say that and leave! What about my hair? I don't want to walk in there looking like a Ringling Brothers clown," cried Jessie. "I don't know what to wear. Help me."

"Those are precisely the words I have been waiting to hear, sister of mine. Now, don't give me any trouble. From this moment on, Jessie Williams, you are in my competent and capable hands." Cass took her arm. "When I am through with you, you won't recognize yourself."

In tow, Jessie muttered, "That's what I'm afraid of."

Barely two hours later, Jess stood in front of the mirror in their bedroom. Cass had made her look—well—pretty. She examined her face. What a difference a little mascara, blush, eye shadow, eyeliner, and lip gloss made.

"My boring brown eyes look big. I never knew my eyelashes were so long. Cass, the lip gloss and blush are perfect!"

"I didn't use much. That's the secret. You have high cheekbones so it is easy to play them up. I like that color of lip gloss on you," explained Cass, tilting Jessie's face one way and then another.

"This hairstyle makes me look older." Cass had

styled her hair, coiling it in a sophisticated chignon with a pretty bow barrette.

Cass put her hands on her hips. "Now let's put it all together."

Jess turned around. Her sister had selected clothes she'd never thought of. A soft pink angora sweater with a scooped neck, and black jeans. Elegant gold hoops and a matching bangle bracelet completed the outfit. Even the black suede flats studded with small gold balls worked.

"Oh, Cass, thanks so much! I never could have done all of this for myself," said Jessie, her eyes shining. Mom had been right. She could see some of Mom's beauty in her face.

"Stand in front of the mirror and turn around. I want to put some hair spray on you. Oh! And dab your wrists and throat with my perfume. Remember, just stay relaxed. If you don't know what to say, smile."

"Thanks, Cass. Will all of this help me if I can't dance?"

"Trust me. Just follow the basic steps. Do what your partner does. Get your jacket. That's probably Joe ringing the doorbell now. And you're welcome, Jess. I had more fun doing this than you'll ever know."

As they neared OPA, Jess's confidence faltered. She crouched in the back seat of the car. Before she knew it, they were there. With a promise to pick her up at ten o'clock, Joe and Cass drove off.

The Oakland Performing Arts Middle School loomed before Jess. She wasn't the only one standing

and staring at it. Addie Mae was a few feet ahead of
her. She had on a black leather skirt and a green sweatshirt with a huge black fist in the center. Her hair was
braided. Leather cutouts of the continent of Africa
hung from her ears and her neck. Jessie wondered if
Addie Mae dressed like a political poster when she
climbed into bed each night.

"So, you going in?"

Addie Mae turned around. "Do we have a choice?"

Both girls took a deep breath and moved closer to
one another as they entered the building. They exchanged anxious smiles. The two fighting African-
American girls wordlessly joined forces. Both squared
their shoulders and, matching step for step, they entered the dance.

The lunchroom/auditorium was unrecognizable.
Multicolored lights flashed. A rap group belted out
some song. Balloons in the school colors of red and
green bobbed above them. Clusters of students milled
about. Teachers circulated. Jessie smelled food. Her
stomach lurched.

The boys clustered on one side of the room and the
girls on the other. Jessie saw some couples dancing but
not nearly as many as she'd imagined. Girls were dancing with each other. Cass hadn't mentioned this.

By silent agreement, Jessie and Addie May stayed
together. They scanned the crowds for Julie and Maria.
In a short time they found them. Maria was dancing
with a boy. Julie sat on one of the few empty chairs.

"Hey, Julie, how long have you been here?"

"Too long, Jessie. I want to go home," she said. "But I can't until my mother comes back."

"Why isn't your father coming to pick you up?" Addie Mae's voice was sharp.

Julie flushed. "He's not feeling well."

"Oh, I see," Addie Mae said. "What the heck is going on with you, Julie?"

"Addie Mae, don't get started," warned Jessie.

"Don't call me that! You know my name, Jessie."

Jessie wondered if she should tell what she knew about the real Addie Mae. Then she decided what was good enough for Mr. Reynolds was . . .

"I'll just call you Cooper, until you figure out who you are."

"I know who I am. Leave me alone." Addie Mae marched off.

Jessie decided to take the plunge. "Julie, why did you act so weird at my house? Is it something to do with me or my family?"

"*No.* I like your family. Your house is great," Julie said, her eyes huge. "It's just that . . ."

"Just what? Look, Julie, you've acted strange since the first day in class. What's wrong? Even my mother is concerned."

Julie looked off. "I can't talk about it yet. When I do I get crazy."

But Jessie wasn't taking that for an answer. "Julie, you are one of the Fours. We're supposed to learn how to be a family. You can trust me."

"You can't tell anybody, Jessie. You have to promise that." A steel cable threaded its way into Julie's voice.

"I promise."

"You mean it."

"Yes."

"We, I mean, my father and mother and little brother, used to live in the hills. About a mile from where you live. You don't remember me, but I went to Scott Elementary with you for a while. We weren't in the same room."

Jessie's head whirled. *Julie knew me from Scott. If she lived about a mile from the house then—*

Julie lowered her head. It was difficult to hear her. "Yeah, you got it. Our house burned in the fire. We lost everything."

"Oh, Julie, I'm so sorry. I didn't know. I would never have been so pushy if I'd known," said Jessie.

"That's OK," she murmured. "You're the first person I ever told. I think Maria knows. She's smart. I think she figured it out."

"Did everybody get out safely?"

Julie nodded. "All my family did. We could see the flames on our roof as we ran down the street. Our car exploded."

"I don't know what to say. At least nobody got hurt."

Julie started to cry softly. "No, not everybody got out alive. I lost my—" She stopped.

"What? Your what?"

"I can't talk anymore, Jessie. It's too hard," she whispered, getting up. "My head aches. I'm going to find a quiet room to sit in."

Jessie fidgeted. "No, stay here. I'll go get us something to drink. I'll be right back. Don't move." Jessie willed the girl to stay where she was. She couldn't let Julie run away—not now.

"Here's money. Thanks, Jess."

"Keep it. Your treat next time."

Jessie made her way to the other side of the room. Some of the boys were actually paying attention to her. Cass was a miracle worker. Julie's secret scared her. The horrors of the fire lurked inside, ready to leap out.

No wonder Julie Stone is so sad. Maybe our group can do something to help her. But I promised to keep her secret. What should I do?

A boy jostled her arm. Jessie moved on. There behind the table, selling soda pop, was Jamar. She'd think about Julie later.

"Hey, there you are! I've been wondering where you were. You really look pretty. Want some pop? What kind?" he asked.

Jessie swallowed. "I didn't know you were in the Student Council. Two orange sodas and a bag of potato chips."

He grinned. "I have to get political experience wherever I can. I'll be on duty another half hour. You look pretty, Jessie. Oh, I'm repeating myself. So what, you look great! I'll find you and we can dance."

"I was hoping you forgot about that."

"No way. Here you go." He waited, handing her the sodas.

"Look, Jamar, you know I don't dance that well," she mumbled.

He laughed. "Neither do I, so we'll do fine."

Shaking her head, Jessie wove her way through couples to the side of the room. Relieved, she saw Julie. She handed her the drink.

"Thanks, Jessie. Please don't tell the others what I told you."

Jess groped for the right words. "Listen, Julie, whatever I can do to help, I will. I mean, even though our house didn't burn, it was terrible. I know it is much worse for you. But at least you can have some fun for a few hours. And you can talk to me whenever you need to."

Julie placed the can of soda pop on the floor. "I do feel better. You go ahead and dance. I like watching."

At that moment a tall boy with long blond hair stood in front of Julie.

"Hi? Want to dance?" he asked.

"She sure does!" replied Jessie, pulling Julie up and pushing her forward.

As they walked off, Julie turned and silently mouthed, "I'll get you for this, Jessie Williams."

"Time to dance."

Somehow Jamar had managed to edge around her. Without waiting, he took her arm and led her into the crowd of moving kids.

"OK, Jessie. Just follow me."

Jessie recalled what Cass had told her. She watched Jamar move in time to the music, his arms pumping. Before long Jess had managed to relax enough to imitate him. Pretending that she was miming his movements made dancing easier. She snapped her fingers and grinned.

"You got it!" he said.

Jessie smiled wider.

By the end of the evening, Jessie had danced with Jamar seven times. Jamar could dance circles around her, but she was learning fast. A few feet away she saw Addie Mae with a boy who was wearing a Malcolm X sweatshirt. It was a rare sight to see that angry girl grinning. She could really dance. Maria was standing with her parents. As far as Jessie could tell only one boy had been brave enough to approach Maria. And Julie was dancing and talking and grinning—all at the same time—with that blond-haired boy!

"Jessie, let me show you this step!"

"Jamar Lewis! I have a feeling you know how to dance!"

Jamar smiled at her. The beat thundered. As they danced, Jess wished that the dance would never end.

chapter

6

"So, tell me everything." Cassandra sat on the bed, her eyes wide and expectant.

Jessie sank into the pillows. "Cass, it was a dream come true! I felt pretty! Thank you so much."

"I had a lot to work with, Jess. Mom helped me when I went to my first dance. I wanted to be the one who helped you," said Cass. "So you had fun?"

"Jamar asked me to dance seven times! Five fast dances and two slow ones! I only stumbled five times. Addie Mae had a good time. But Maria's parents hung around her." Jessie clasped one of the pillows close. "Julie wanted to sit the dance out, but I stopped that. I made her dance with this boy who asked her. He danced with her all night."

Someone knocked on the door.

Both sisters yelled, "Come in!"

"We want the whole report from beginning to end," said Mamatoo, with their mother behind her carrying a tray.

"Here's milk and cookies, just like when you two were my little girls," said Mrs. Williams. "I look at the two of you and realize that I don't have little girls anymore."

"Move over, Jessie. Make room for two ex–party girls! Daughter, don't go getting sentimental and weepy. These children have to grow up the same way you did." Mamatoo snatched an oatmeal and raisin cookie.

"I realize that, Mother. But to have my Jessie going to her first dance? Next thing, she'll be dating."

"And then Jessie goes away to college. Far, far away. Next, acting school. Soon she is a great actress on Broadway. Falls in love. Marries. Has four children— all upstart, brash girls like her and—"

Mrs. Williams threw her hands up. "Mother, please!"

Mamatoo winked at the sisters. "Jess, make room for me on that bed."

Surprised, Jessie obeyed her grandmother. They were treating her as special. Nobody was comparing her to Cass! They were listening to her! For the next hour, conversation and giggles flowed around the bed. Gradually, Jessie nodded off. She hardly felt her mother's kiss.

Over the weekend Jessie practiced her part as the Old Woman in the African Cinderella story. Jess counted the number of words in her part. Exactly fifty-three.

Sunday came too soon. Books stacked, ready for school, Jessie surveyed her closet. She had rearranged the closet, organizing her clothes by color. Just like her sister.

"That looks good. Now you can mix and match by color," said Cass, sorting through her jewelry.

"I have too much red."

They both laughed.

"You know what, Jess? I feel like a real big sister," Cass said. "I love it! After I finish with the jewelry, I'll go through my clothes. I hope there's something you like. Check out this pile. Take your pick."

Earrings, bracelets, and necklaces glittered. "Cass, you put your gold hoops in here. The ones you let me wear to the back-to-school dance."

Cass picked them up. "I know. I want you to have them."

"But you worked in the bookstore for months to buy these. I remember," protested Jessie.

Cass smiled. "Dad was a royal pain. Look, if I bought them, I can give them to anyone I want to. And I want to give them to you."

"Why, Cass? Why don't you want to keep them? Why give them to me?"

Her sister wandered over to the window. "I keep

trying to forget the day of the fire. But I can't. I see Dad's hand, listen to my friends, look outside—and it all comes back. I enjoy having pretty jewelry, but on that day I didn't care about things. Just our family."

"I know a girl who got burned out. She's nice. I wish I could help her," said Jessie, thinking of Julie Stone.

"Having you as a friend is a help to her, Jess. Let me give you the earrings. They looked so pretty on you the night of the dance. If I need to wear them, I'll borrow them back. Here." Cass placed the shining hoops in Jessie's hands.

"But I don't have anything to give you, Cass. Your birthday isn't until April," said Jessie, holding the hoops in the palm of her hand.

"Yes you do," said Cass, her voice soft. "I watch you and see me when I started sixth grade. Everything is new. You have so much going for you, Jess. Not just looks, but real talent."

"Not everybody thinks so," replied Jessie.

"Then they're ignorant and blind and nuts and not worth a dime."

Would Cass say that about Mrs. Grant, her favorite fifth-grade teacher? Jessie's mind raced.

"*Anybody* who said mean things about me?" asked Jessie.

Cass didn't miss a beat. "Anybody on this planet."

"Even Mrs. Grant?"

"My old fifth-grade teacher? You bet. She's included. So is Dad. *Anybody*, Jess, and I mean it."

A narrow, deep crack began to split the wall inside Jessie. For almost two years, that wall had protected her from some of the pain of that day and helped her keep the secret. But even cracked, the wall remained.

"What's the gift I can give you?" Jess suddenly asked.

"Promise to be my friend. Not because of how I look or my grades or my being a cheerleader. Promise to love me even when I'm not perfect," said Cass.

"I promise. I'll be your friend, Cass. I promise. Please don't run off and get married to Joe." Jess grinned. "Unless you take me with you as your maid of honor. And all three of us go to Hawaii for the honeymoon."

"You got a deal. Now let me see you with the earrings on again."

Jess put them on. She danced around their bedroom. "These will be my good-luck earrings. I'll wear them to every audition and opening night. Thanks, Cass."

True to her word, Jessie wore the gold hoops when she got dressed Monday morning. She ran to Family Hour. Mr. Reynolds reviewed the major events for the week. It was becoming clear that life at OPA ran only on one track—the fast track. Presentations in each of the performing arts were sprinkled throughout the week.

"Find out when members of your group will be performing or showing their work. See them perform this week. Learning about each other's talents is a class requirement." Mr. Reynolds emphasized the last sentence.

By the end of the half hour, Jessie had jotted down the times to see Addie Mae dance and hear Julie and Maria play at different recitals. With Mr. Reynolds's "Make it a good day" ringing in her ears, Jessie floated through the morning. In a few hours, she would be the Old Woman in her first reader's theater part. *Life is full of surprises*, she thought.

Jessie arrived at the theater early. It was full. When the lights dimmed, conversation stopped. On cue, Jessie walked out with the cast and took her place before her stand, fourth from the right. She lifted the *kente* cloth panel and draped it over her left shoulder. On cue, she took her seat. Sylvia Duncan, the narrator, spoke. Jessie forgot about the audience. She became the Old Woman, in a magical forest in ancient Africa.

A full moon, round as a silver balloon, hung above her. She sat on the cold stone. It was late. In the distance, quick footsteps came her way, just as she knew they would.

It was Manyara, Nyasha's selfish, mean sister. Manyara was running through the forest bound to get to the king before her sister. Bound and determined to win his heart and become queen. The Old Woman spoke, her hand reaching out.

"Manyara, child, please stop and listen to me."

The girl's voice was impatient and harsh. "How do you know who I am?"

"Oh, I know. I know many things. I am here to help you. Listen to my advice. It will help you win your heart's desire. Soon after you pass the place where—" The Old Woman spoke in a clear, strong voice.

Proud Manyara interrupted. "Be quiet, Old Woman! You are talking to your future queen!"

The play ended too soon for Jess. Applause and whistles from the audience filled the air around her. Mr. Reynolds and Miss Baker clapped, as the cast bowed their heads. The curtain lowered.

"Jessie, you were really good."

"Thanks, Jamar."

"Hey, Jessie, nice work. Hi, Jamar." River batted her eyes in mock adoration. "You were the best king I've ever seen. Maybe we'll be in the Harriet Tubman play together."

They laughed.

When Jessie headed out, she saw Addie Mae waiting for her.

"Jessie, I never heard of that story. It wasn't like the Walt Disney version. Much more interesting. You were . . ." Addie Mae paused, "convincing. Shoot, you were impressive, Jessie. Look, I am scheduled to dance after school. Then we're supposed to meet and go to the Evergreen Residential Manor. I'll hurry to meet you all."

"No problem. Thanks for coming to see me, Cooper. I'll be there to see you dance."

"You will? I have to go." Addie Mae hurried off.

It was exhilarating to hear strangers say, "You were good. What's your name?" Jessie spent the rest of the afternoon sailing on a cloud. By the time she reached the dance theater, the doors had closed. Jessie sneaked in and sat on the steps. She looked for Maria and Julie, but it was too packed.

The African Dance Troupe performed three dances. Addie Mae was in the second line. Two boys and a girl began beating out a complex combination of rhythms on large drums. The front line of dancers started to sway and move. Each of the remaining three lines followed.

Above the drums, the cries from the dancers heightened the excitement. Jessie concentrated on Addie Mae. The girl had real talent. She belonged in the first line. She moved with such precision and grace. Jessie shook her head. She'd had no idea that Addie Mae was so gifted. When the performance ended, Jessie stood up with the rest of the audience. The three girls waited for Addie Mae after the performance.

Jessie stepped forward. "Cooper, you were great! I mean it."

Addie Mae/Mkiwa blushed.

Maria added, "It was beautiful and you were so good, Cooper."

"Thanks, Maria. Thanks, Jessie."

"I never knew how good you are, Cooper," Julie said, her eyes bright. "It seems like all of us are calling you Cooper, like Mr. Reynolds. I don't want to offend you."

"Thanks for thinking about me. Cooper is fine—just don't call me Addie Mae," she said.

Together they left for Evergreen Residential Manor. It was a long, one-story building with a redwood shingle roof. A wide ramp ran down one side of the building. Maria led the way in. Jessie didn't know what to expect. A woman sat at a counter before them, reading. To their right, she heard the sounds of barking dogs, meowing cats, and talking birds.

"Hello. My name is Maria Hernandez. These are my friends. We made an appointment to talk with Mrs. Winters about our community project."

"Yes, she is expecting you. Mrs. Winters is in the dayroom, but she should be with you in a few minutes," said the woman. "Have a seat."

Everybody did, except for Julie. She walked over to the noisy room and went in. After a minute, Addie Mae followed her. Then, Maria. Jessie waited for them to come out. When they didn't, she finally peeked in. The room was large and airy, with green plants hanging from the ceiling. Elderly people, some in wheelchairs, were playing with an odd assortment of animals. Julie was holding a cat.

"What's going on?" Jessie asked Maria.

Maria patted a small terrier. "Come on in. The county has a special program where they bring in animals for a day each month for the seniors to play with. It's good for morale. My mother told me about it."

"Julie really loves cats."

Maria followed Jessie's eyes. Julie caressed a large

gray cat. She was talking to it. An elderly woman chatted with her. Addie Mae sat by an elderly black man, talking her head off. He nodded his head and listened. Her face glowed.

"Look at the two of them. Does this place have some kind of magic spell or something?" asked Maria. "We're supposed to be here helping these people. They don't act like they need any help."

"Your mother said that our plan was good," said Jessie. "I think we should talk to Mrs. Winters. The worst we can do is to make them happier."

"Excuse me. I'm Mrs. Winters. Would you like to go into my office so we can talk?"

Both girls stared at a short, professional-looking woman with very short black hair. Forty minutes later the schedule was arranged. The girls would perform on Wednesday, October 14. Then every other week they would spend thirty to forty minutes entertaining the seniors.

Besides watching Maria and Julie perform, Jessie prepared for the auditions for the big Winter Festival play about Harriet Tubman. By the weekend, she had rehearsed with Mamatoo and reread the play a dozen times.

Jessie sighed. Her head spun at the thought of winning the lead role. *Imagine me as the great freedom fighter Harriet Tubman! There I would stand, in front of a group of my enslaved people. They would be waiting for me to lead them to freedom in the North. In my hand is a huge pistol. Loaded with fat lead bullets.*

The bedroom faded away. Darkness, thick as fog, a slice of moon, and chilly damp air surrounded her. The hoots of an owl and muted sobs were the only sounds. Hundreds of miles separated her small group from freedom. The threat of capture and death lurked behind every tree and bush.

An argument broke out. Terrified of possible capture, two of their number insisted on turning back. But Harriet never allowed anyone to do that. That's what the pistol was for. She'd never had to shoot anybody and she hoped she wouldn't have to this trip. Long ago, she had faced that possibility. No one was allowed to go back to slavery. There was always the chance they would be forced to talk. Any information a slave owner got jeopardized Harriet's operation. There was only one road open to them—the perilous road to freedom.

Harriet Tubman pointed the pistol at the shivering young man and woman. "We've got miles to go. Nobody turns their back on freedom. You all are on my Underground Railroad. Every one of my passengers gets a one-way ticket."

There Harriet Tubman stood, one short, dark-skinned woman, her voice deep and dangerous, pistol poised, warning, "Live North or die here!"

Jessie opened her eyes, back in her bedroom. What a courageous person Harriet Tubman was! No wonder she was known as the best conductor on the Underground Railroad.

Jess knew that the Underground Railroad was not an actual train system. It was a series of houses, cabins, shacks, barns, stores, and other places that stretched across states. Many of the brave owners of these dwellings were free African-American families. They as well as others risked their lives each time they took in escaping slaves, fed and hid them. At each stop, directions to the next safe place were given. Each stop on the Underground Railroad was a step further from slavery and closer to freedom, but always a dangerous one. The fact that Harriet Tubman had led so many of her people to freedom astonished Jessie.

Again, she sighed. What a great scene that would be. But not this time. Not this leading role. She wasn't ready for it. But one day she would be.

Her best choice was either Harriet Tubman as a young girl or as an old woman. When she thought about it, even the more interesting of the two roles wasn't very exciting. "I hope I don't get typecast. I don't want to spend my three years at OPA playing old women," Jessie mumbled.

Stacks of books about Harriet Tubman were piled around Jessie. Some were from Dad's bookstore, the rest from the school library. Jessie concentrated on the sections about Harriet as an elderly woman. By the time she was forty-nine or fifty years old, Harriet had guided more than three hundred slaves to freedom and never lost one. She'd made nineteen treacherous trips back South and even freed her parents and siblings. Jessie shook her head as she read about Harriet's Civil War adventures as a spy, a scout, and a hospital nurse, for the Union Army.

Curious, Jessie read on. Harriet Tubman lived until 1913. She died at the age of ninety-three. For years she never got any pay or pension for her dangerous and important work in the Union Army. At last, in 1890, she received a very small amount of money, far below what others who had served got.

Against all odds, this illiterate old woman named Harriet Tubman established a home for any person needing somewhere to stay and rest. *I'll have to get hold of a wheelchair so I can practice*, Jessie thought. Painful rheumatism had forced Harriet into a wheelchair.

Jessie closed the book. So much to work on. Tryouts for her part and three others started on Thursday. *At least I have company. All the other Fours are faced with big auditions, too. We were lucky the first time around, but how well will we do for the big ones?*

During the week of auditions, Mr. Reynolds shook his head in amazement at the Fours. Maria drifted in humming and moving her fingers up and down an imaginary piano. Julie sawed her bow against an imaginary violin, running her fingers along invisible strings. Addie Mae glided, swayed, tapped her feet, and moved her body in a series of patterns. Jessie spoke with a Southern accent, pretending that she couldn't read or write and walking as if she were ninety-three years old. Morning. Noon. And night.

Tuesday night, as Jessie struggled to complete the sets of equations before her, she was pleased with her final practice session with Mamatoo. Jessie swallowed.

She was thirsty. When she stood up to go get some water, she tripped.

"Jess, are you feeling all right? You look tired." Cass placed her hand on her sister's forehead. "And you feel warm."

"Cass, I can't get sick. Day after tomorrow I audition for the Harriet Tubman play." Jessie's voice squeaked.

"Climb into bed. I'll get you some water and aspirin. At least you've stopped talking like you were born and bred in the pre–Civil War South!" teased Cass.

Jessie undressed and buttoned her pajamas. "Cass, you have to understand that being an actress is very serious, disciplined work. I have to live my character."

"Stop talking! I'll bring a box of salt down so you can gargle. That should help your throat. You sound hoarse." Cass left.

Before Jessie crawled into bed, she put on the gold hoops Cass had given her. *One good night's sleep and I'll be fine.*

When Jess woke up on Wednesday morning, her throat hurt. She gargled with salt and warm water. Cass clucked in sympathy and handed her two aspirin. Getting to school was difficult. Everything ached. She tried to hurry to Home Base.

Mr. Reynolds called the roll. "Cooper?"

There was no answer.

"Cooper?"

Addie Mae jerked up out of her dance trance. "Here, Mr. Reynolds."

"You four girls have more determination than I've seen in many years. I'm going to name you The Gotta-Be's," he joked.

The Family Hour class hooted their approval.

Jessie raised her hand. "Mr. Reynolds, we are The Do-Be's!" She started to say more, but her throat really hurt. She felt hot. *Oh, no, I can't get a cold!*

"You don't sound good," commented Addie Mae.

"I think I'm getting a cold. My throat feels raw," Jessie admitted.

"Don't take any of that cold medicine. When you get home, soak a towel in hot water. You got an aloe vera plant? Good. Cut off some of the stalks. Slit them open and rub your throat with the juice from them. Then put the towel around your neck." She took a breath. "Squeeze two lemons into a cup, add two teaspoons of honey, fill the cup with hot water. Drink as many of those as you can."

"Then float away," joked Maria.

"Thanks a lot, you two. Maybe it's just nerves."

Later that morning, Jessie was next to Julie when the accident happened. They were hurrying upstairs for their math/science core class. Helplessly, Jessie watched as Julie tripped and fell backward. The violin case slid down the stairs. As Julie tried to catch the railing, she cried out. Her right leg was twisted beneath her. Julie tumbled down five steps.

By the time the ambulance came, Jessie was in tears. Julie had hurt her leg—badly. Julie's parents would meet her at the hospital. Jessie squeezed her hand.

"Jessie, what about my audition?" Julie whispered.

"Don't worry. I'll talk to Mr. Reynolds. He'll make sure you get a chance to audition as soon as you can come back to school."

Julie moaned. "Thanks, Jessie."

In Family Hour, the class wrote get-well cards. Mr. Reynolds promised to take care of the audition problem. Before they left, the girls called the hospital. They would not release any news about Julie.

"Don't worry. We've got her home phone number," said Maria. "Keep trying and whoever gets news first, calls the others."

Addie Mae and Jessie agreed.

Still feeling achy, Jessie rushed home. She hurried to the telephone. On her fifth try, she got Julie's mother. Julie had a badly sprained right ankle. She would be on crutches. The hospital was keeping her for a couple of days to rule out the possibility of a concussion.

"Thank you girls so much for calling. I'll tell Julie that she can still audition. That will cheer her up," said Mrs. Stone.

"Good. When will she be back at school?" rasped Jessie. Her voice was scratchy.

"Hopefully, by Monday. Sometimes Julie can be quite stubborn. She told me that nothing could stop her from being back by the fourteenth when you do your community project."

Recalling that the fire had destroyed Julie's home compelled Jessie to speak out. "Mrs. Stone, I . . . well, our house almost got burned down in the fire. Is there anything I can do, I mean . . ."

"That's considerate of you, Jessie. Going from a big house to a small apartment hasn't been easy. We're doing as well as can be expected, though. I appreciate your asking. Oh! Thank you for pushing Julie to have fun at the school dance. Mike calls her every day!" said Mrs. Stone.

"You mean the boy with the blond hair?"

Mrs. Stone was quiet. "We haven't met him yet. He is the boy Julie danced with most of the night?"

"The only one! That's good news!"

"My, I may have made a big mistake. I thought Julie had told you about him. Please don't say anything to her unless she brings it up. This is one of the first times I feel like I'm getting my spunky, unpredictable daughter back," explained Julie's mother.

"You can count on me. My lips are sealed," Jessie promised. "Thanks, Mrs. Stone. Tell Julie we all want her to get well soon."

Jessie hung up and telephoned Addie Mae and Maria. Then she got the aloe vera plant and cut off a thick green stalk. She followed Addie Mae's directions. After three cups of hot lemonade and honey, she stopped. *Vitamin C helps. I should drink a little orange juice. Just a tiny bit can't hurt.*

When she woke up on Thursday morning, not only

did Jessie have a weaker voice, but her face had broken out in a rash.

"Oh! I want to die! Cass!" she screamed.

Cass hopped out of bed. "Jess, what did you do? Just don't tell me that you drank orange juice. You know you're allergic to it."

"I was so worried about being sick for the audition, I thought that a little wouldn't hurt," sobbed Jessie. "I can't go to school."

"Oh, yes, you can. You don't have any options. Jess, you put the pressure on Dad to let you go to OPA. You can't cop out now," said Cass. "Talk to Mr. Reynolds. See if you can try out tomorrow."

At breakfast, her mother and father just shook their heads. Mamatoo came upstairs to join the family for morning coffee.

"Oh, my heavens, child, what in the world have you gone and done?" said her grandmother, holding Jessie's chin in her hand. "Looks like one of your allergic rashes. That won't stop you from auditioning."

Jessie moaned. "You can't mean it, Mamatoo! Audition, looking like this?"

"Exactly. You can't let inconsequential mistakes in judgment stop you."

In school, Jessie hid her face as much as possible. The bumps felt as if they were getting larger and larger. If she was lucky she wouldn't see Jamar. That would be too much to bear. Her feet dragged as she rounded the corner to Home Base.

Mr. Reynolds stood at the door.

"Miss Williams, you are not at your peak, I see."

Jessie struggled to hold back the tears, but it was difficult. "Mr. Reynolds, I need a gigantic favor."

"Jessie, please don't talk anymore. Rest your voice and don't worry about your face. You aren't auditioning your face. Let's see how you are tomorrow afternoon. How's that?"

Jessie wanted to hug him. "You are the best teacher in the whole world. Thanks."

When Addie Mae danced in, Jessie turned her head away.

"Wow! What happened?"

"Cooper, don't you dare make fun of me!"

"Why would I do that?" Addie Mae's face crumbled faster than a cookie in a two-year-old's hands. "I'm not mean like you seem to think I am, Jessie."

Maria interrupted, "Stop it, you two. Jessie, be quiet. We'll talk for you."

"Attention, please. You have to complete an exercise. In your groups, develop a family tree for each member. We'll do a class chart at the end and discover where we come from and what our families are like," instructed the teacher.

"It's my turn to be leader. Cooper, what about you?" Maria took out a sheet of paper and started writing. "Let's do Jessie last. Now, what's your father's name?"

Addie Mae/Mkiwa twisted in her seat. "My father's name is James Cooper."

"And your mother?"

Addie Mae drummed her fingers on the desk top. "Evelyn Collins Cooper."

"How many brothers and sisters do you have?"

Mkiwa seemed about to cry.

"Wait a minute. Cooper, what's wrong?" Maria stopped writing.

"I don't want to do this."

Jessie looked up. Addie Mae was getting more and more distraught.

"Come on, we have to. How many brothers?" pressed Maria.

"One. I mean, none."

Maria looked puzzled. "Stop playing around, Cooper. You never talk about your family. This is an easy question. None, one, two, three, more?"

Addie Mae twisted her braids. "None. None at all. Not any. Zip. Zero."

"Have it your way, Cooper," said Maria. "I'll go next. I have two older brothers. They are identical twins. And I . . . well, let me go to my aunts and uncles and cousins."

Jess listened as Maria talked. Something about Maria's sharing bothered her. But she couldn't figure out what it was. As for Cooper, Maria was correct. They knew next to nothing about Addie Mae's family, other than that her mother worked at a hospital and her father worked double and triple shifts as a fireman so he was hardly ever home. Something was wrong. Really wrong. But what?

At the end of the day, Jessie headed for the tryouts. Even though she wasn't after the part of Harriet Tubman, she needed to check out her competition. Mamatoo advised against doing that, but this time Jessie had to. She eased the door open and snuck into a seat in the back on the far left-hand side of the theater.

Just as River had said, Sylvia Duncan was trying out for the role of Harriet Tubman as a young woman—the meatiest part in the play. Jessie had to admit that she was outstanding. Sylvia didn't resemble Harriet in any way. She wasn't dark-skinned or small, but she managed to create an aura of gutsy resolve. She had mastered the accent and dialect. Mr. Reynolds had told them that they would not be casting the play based on race alone. One white girl read for the leading role. *She's not half bad*, Jessie mused.

There were six girls trying out for the part of Harriet as an old woman, the part that Jessie wanted. Two of them would be hard to beat. Both were older and more experienced. Jessie sank into her seat.

Where is Jamar? We only bump into each other in the hall, except for improv class, but that ends after next week. I hope he takes beginning drama with me. But Jamar wasn't there. Her spirits hit the floor, though why she'd want Jamar to see her looking like an acne advertisement was hard to figure out.

I miss seeing him, Jess admitted to herself on the bus ride home.

Jessie went to bed trying to believe that her voice would be strong by Friday afternoon. As for the rash on her face, Mr. Reynolds was right. *I'm not auditioning my face.* Exhausted, she drifted off to sleep. During the night, she hardly moved.

"Jessie! Jessie! It's time to go to school. Hey, sister, wake up. Can you talk?"

"Morning, Cass. My voice is better!" Jessie rolled over. "Is my face cleared up?"

Cass patted her shoulder. "Not yet, but it will be, Jess."

"But Cass, this is the day I audition for a part in the Winter Festival play."

Her sister sighed. "Wear the gold hoop earrings, your blue jeans, and that red T-shirt. I'll send you good vibes."

By the end of the day, Jessie was resigned to having to get up in front of her fellow students with red hair, a chicken-pox face, and a dull headache, and audition for a role she didn't really want.

The journey to the theater stretched like an endless roadway. Jessie took it step by step. It was an hour before her name was called. Just as she got up, a hand gripped her shoulder from behind.

"Oh, Mamatoo, you came!"

"Now, where do you think I'd be on the afternoon my grandbaby is trying out for her first big part at this fancy school?" chuckled her grandmother, resplendent in a long African gown and head wrap.

"Thanks, Mamatoo. I need you here. I'm wearing my good-luck T-shirt, blue jeans, and the gold earrings Cass gave me."

Buoyed by her grandmother's support, Jessie stood up. Jamar came in.

"I was afraid I'd be too late to see you. Break a leg, Jess. I know you can do it." He sat down next to her grandmother and introduced himself.

Jessie's hands flew to her face. Flustered, she gazed at her shoes.

"Hey, Jess, you look fine. Go get the part!" His eyes shone.

"Now, this is a young man after my own heart. Well, child, go on up there and get that part. Make me proud of you, Jess. Break a leg!" urged Mamatoo.

"I'll do my best." Jessie forced a smile. Only she knew that the smile was fake.

chapter

7

Every eye in the theater watched Jessie. She climbed the stairs to the stage. Jessie tried to focus on Harriet Tubman, old, but still vibrant. She willed herself to forget the people in the audience, the stagelights, and the fear inside. Jessie positioned herself downstage center. She faced the audience. Her heart pounded.

Mr. Reynolds and Miss Baker sat in the fourth row with two other teachers. They whispered as they took notes. Students in the audience were quiet. Jessie could barely see Mamatoo and Jamar in the back. She held the script in her hands.

"Miss Williams, please turn to page 96 and begin reading from the top," directed Mr. Reynolds.

For Jessie it was the longest twenty minutes in her life. Something was wrong. She didn't feel connected

to her character. The committee had her read the parts
of Harriet as a young girl, one of Harriet's sisters, and a
free black woman whose house served as a station on
the Underground Railroad.

"Thank you, Miss Williams. The results will be
posted by Wednesday." Miss Baker called the name of
the next student.

"What happened to you up there?" Mamatoo asked.

Jessie frowned. "I don't know. I just couldn't get
into it."

"You weren't bad," said Jamar. "I read for the part of
Harriet's first husband. Maybe I'll get it and then
again, maybe I won't. At least I tried."

Jessie managed a wan smile. "Thanks, Jamar. I
didn't do my best and they knew it. I'll be lucky to
paint scenery."

Mamatoo and Jessie rode home. Outside the wind
whistled. Fall leaves plucked from their branches scattered about the streets. Away from the fire-scarred
hills, the autumn foliage was striking.

A searing red tree caught Jessie's eye. Scrawny and
fragile, it stood among greens, browns, and dulled yel-
lows. Soon it would be stripped bare, but today each
leaf flamed. Not red-hot and scary like the fire, but
bold and scrappy like a smear on a painter's palette.

As the car drove past the small tree, Jessie turned
around to snatch one final glimpse.

The telephone rang three times that night. Maria,
Addie Mae, and Julie each called to see how the audi-

tion went. Jessie told the ugly truth. Maria confessed that she had botched three chords. And even Addie Mae had been forced to start again when she tripped over her own feet. Julie's audition wasn't until next week. She sounded relieved. Jessie put the telephone down, realizing that auditioning was traumatic for everyone.

Jessie remained by the telephone in the kitchen. Something kept nagging at her. *We have more than the auditions to worry about. Darn! That community project at Evergreen Residential Manor! We have to meet and get ready to present! ASAP!*

Quickly, Jessie dialed Maria. After another round of calls it was agreed that they would meet Sunday afternoon at Maria's to practice for their first performance at Evergreen Residential Manor. Jessie agreed to call Julie.

"But Julie, are you sure you should? I mean, your sprained ankle, plus you still have to audition, and the fire. Seems like too much to me," said Jessie.

"My *hands* aren't sprained, Jess. My father will bring me. I can walk on these dumb crutches," said Julie. "I have to be with you and Cooper and Maria."

Jessie was startled. "You do?"

"Yes, I do. This project is important to me. If we don't stick together like a team, we all get a low grade. But it's more than that. I love going to Evergreen."

"But we can cover for you, Julie."

Julie's voice was firm. "No. We're supposed to be

the Do-Be's. Going there makes me happy. And that guy you made me dance with, remember him?"

"The one with the blond hair?" Jessie acted vague.

"Yeah. His name is Mike Stewart and he calls me every day. He's in sixth grade like us. He plays alto saxophone and loves jazz. I had more fun at the dance than I've had in months. Thanks, Jess."

"You're welcome."

"Life has to get better. And if one miracle could happen . . ." Julie's voice drifted off.

Jessie was instantly alert. "What miracle? Tell me!"

"I've got to go. I can't talk about it now. See you later, Jess."

Jessie headed downstairs. *One long, short, short, short.* No answer. Maybe Mamatoo was taking a bath. Mom was napping. Dad was still at the bookstore. Jessie grabbed a sweater and opened the sliding glass door to the deck.

The deck jutted out over a hill. The awful scars left by the fire were muted in the twilight. The wind blew fierce and cold against her face. Surviving five weeks at the Oakland Performing Arts Middle School had been rough. The next five weeks wouldn't be any easier. Middle-school life moved at a faster pace than she was used to. The stakes were much higher, too.

Without warning, the turmoil and changes of the past forty days flooded over Jessie. Tears held back for weeks spilled over. Her brown hands gripped the deck rail. Red hair, rash, and all, Jessie Williams turned her face full front to the wind. Part of her yearned for the simpler life she had lived before sixth grade. But that time was over. *Watching Cass grow up was a whole lot easier than doing it myself. I didn't know how good I had it then*, Jess said to the bare, dead trees. Shivering, she went back inside.

Jessie worked hard on the script for the group project at the senior citizen home. By late Saturday afternoon, she had four copies of the script she had written for their performance. It was good. Cass had helped her type it out on the computer in their room. Printing it took minutes. A quick run to a copy store had completed her preparations for the meeting.

On Sunday afternoon, Cass drove Jessie to Maria's house for the meeting. A tall, very handsome older boy opened the door. Jessie was surprised when another boy who looked just like the first one flung a brief greeting her way as he ran down the front steps. Then she remembered Maria's family tree—they were identical twins.

Everybody was there. Julie sat on a chair. Her right ankle was wrapped in a support bandage. The crutches rested on the floor beside her. She was holding one of Maria's cats in her lap.

"Hi, Jessie. Thanks again for helping me. And for getting Mr. Reynolds to let me audition next week," she said, stroking the cat.

"You're welcome. How do you feel?"

"Better."

Mrs. Hernandez walked in. She looked anxious. "Maria, has your father come home yet?"

"No, Mama."

"What am I going to do with that man? He works two jobs, seven days a week. When I beg him to rest because of his health, he refuses!" She threw up her hands and left.

The girls stared at Maria.

"Don't say anything about this, but Daddy has angina. Something is wrong with his heart. Stress is bad for him. Mama worries that he may have to go to the hospital again," said Maria, her face grave. "We're all afraid."

"I thought everything was perfect in your family," admitted Addie Mae. "Everything."

Maria looked sad. "Cooper, nobody has a perfect family."

Addie Mae closed her mouth. Julie stared at the floor. Jessie concentrated on her feet. The silence thickened. No one knew what to say. Finally, Maria got up and walked over to Julie.

"Miranda never lets anybody hold her. You must have a gift."

Julie smiled. "I love cats."

"Do you have any?" Jessie asked.

When she saw Julie's eyes swell with tears, she wished that she had kept her mouth shut. The last thing she wanted to do was to make her cry.

"I'm sorry. I didn't mean to upset you."

"I know."

Maria coughed. "Let's go to work. We have to be ready for the seniors at Evergreen in three days! Julie, you can't play the violin and hold Miranda."

Jessie passed out copies of the script. The afternoon sped by. The vibrant sounds of the piano, violin, Jessie's voice as Sojourner Truth, or taped African drum music for Addie Mae filled the room. They took a break to eat and then returned to practice.

Maria and Cooper took photographs as part of their presentation to the Family Hour class. Before they left, the girls agreed to meet in the music room after school on Monday and Tuesday to practice. Maria's mother promised to be at the residential home on Wednesday to videotape them.

On Wednesday the results of the auditions were posted at various places in the school. Crowds of students gathered around. Groans and whoops of joy were heard up and down the corridors of OPA.

Jessie hung back. At last she got the courage to read the list by the theater door. The part of the elderly Harriet Tubman had gone to Dorothy Foster. Jessie bit her bottom lip. Sylvia Duncan was listed after "Harriet Tubman as a young woman." *That figures.* And Jamar had been selected as Harriet's second husband. Jessie searched for any mention of her name. There it was. The part of Harriet's sister, Mary Ann, went to Jessie Williams.

"Hey. How did you do?" Jamar stood behind her.

Unable to respond, Jessie fled down the hall. What could she tell Dad, Mom, Cass, and Mamatoo? She was a failure. At the front of the school building she saw the other three.

"I didn't get the part of Harriet as an old woman. I got the part of Harriet's younger sister," said Jessie, the words coming out in a rush. "And I wore all of my good-luck clothes and jewelry!"

Tears glistened in Maria's eyes. "I practiced three hours a day! No matter what else I want to do—I practice and then I fall apart!"

"Maria, it can't be that bad!" said Julie, leaning against the wall, one crutch on the floor.

"I tried out for a simple solo part in the Winter Festival concert. Instead I get to play one song that a two-year-old could play, with the rest of the orchestra!" Maria wiped at the tears falling from her eyes.

"Here." Mkiwa handed her some Kleenex. "Maria, everybody blows it sometimes. Even me. Try being placed in not the first, not the second, but the third line of dancers! My mother will be disappointed, but I know that my father will understand. He's always in my corner. No matter what."

The girls just stared at her.

Jessie decided to let any questions about Addie Mae and her family drop. Everybody waited for Julie to say something.

"I don't feel bad. I get to play a short solo. Nothing really exciting. But to tell the truth, I was surprised and happy. I didn't expect to get to do much of anything," she said.

"Like my grandmother says, 'There's always next time.' And next time we'll do better. I'm glad we all tried." Jessie struggled to sound upbeat.

"I feel the same way, Jessie." Maria handed Julie her crutch.

Jessie bit her bottom lip. "Anyway, we have other opportunities. There's the Spring Fund-Raiser. That's the one that counts the most."

"We don't have time to stand around here," said Addie Mae.

Maria nodded. "They're expecting us at Evergreen in fifteen minutes. If we mess this up, there goes our grade."

"I don't feel much like performing," Jessie confessed.

"We have to." Julie added, as she limped off, "If we're serious artists we have to work even when we don't want to."

The girls carried Julie's things with their own. She walked well on the crutches. The sky was overcast. The chill in the air hurried them along.

Once inside Evergreen Residential Manor, they stowed their belongings in a small room off the day-room. Mrs. Winters had arranged the furniture in the dayroom. Mrs. Hernandez rushed in with the video camera. The girls changed clothes. They had decided to dress up and appear as professional as possible.

Jessie broke the silence. "Julie's right. Professionals give their best, no matter what," she said.

Addie Mae spoke up. "Let's put our hands on top of each other's and say—"

"Four, three, two, one. We're the best. Let's have some fun!" Jessie quipped.

"I like it!" Maria put her hand out.

One after the other they placed their hands on top of each other's. The girls chanted, "Four, three, two, one. We're the best. Let's have some fun!"

Residents and members of the staff crowded the dayroom. The senior citizens sat on chairs or couches, or in wheelchairs. The Fours walked out to smiles and applause. Mrs. Winters introduced them. There was more applause.

The girls took their places. Julie sat on a chair, holding her violin. Her green taffeta dress shimmered. Maria, dressed in a long velvet skirt and white blouse, stood by the piano. Clad in a black bodysuit with a leopard print skirt and head wrap, Addie Mae crouched down on the side. Jessie had on the same black pants, white T-shirt, and *kente* cloth scarf she had worn for the reader's theater performance. The gold hoop earrings glowed against her skin.

"Good afternoon, Evergreen residents. My name is Jessie Williams. My friends and I are sixth graders at the Oakland Performing Arts Middle School. We are very happy to be here. Each one of us has a special dream and talent. We want to share each of our stories with you. Our first Dreamgirl is Maria Hernandez. No one works harder than Maria to make her dream come true. When she succeeds she will open another door for her people." She nodded to Maria, who stepped forward. Jess moved back.

"My name is Maria Hernandez. I live a few blocks from here. When I was five years old, my godmother took me to a piano recital in Mexico City. I saw a beautiful lady sit down at a huge grand piano. The concert hall looked like a castle and she was the queen. She started to play and minutes later I was lost in the most wonderful, magical music I had ever heard in my life. It all came from her mind and hands. When I told my father I wanted to learn how to be a concert pianist, he said that it was not a wise choice. There were few, if any, Mexican female concert pianists. But my godmother and mother persuaded him to let me take piano lessons."

Maria moved to the piano. "My dream is to become a world-class concert pianist. I will now play the audition piece that won me entrance into the castle, the Oakland Performing Arts Middle School." More applause filled the room. Maria nodded.

The lilting strains of the *New World Symphony* flowed over the audience. Jessie listened closely. Maria wasn't making any mistakes. Mrs. Hernandez videotaped the presentation. When Maria finished and took her place by the side of the piano, the room shook with approval. More relaxed, Jessie walked to the center of the room.

"Our next Dreamgirl is Mkiwa Cooper. She has chosen a rough road to dance on. Her heroines represent the most brilliant shining stars in the world of dance. When she succeeds she will continue the legacy they have left behind for her people." Jessie nodded to Addie Mae as she turned on the taped music. African drums and percussion instruments created an exciting mood.

"My name is Mkiwa Cooper. All of my life I have wanted to be a dancer like Judith Jamison of the Alvin Ailey Dance Company. For years I have taken classes in ballet, tap, modern dance, and African dance. I continue to take classes on Saturdays and practice every day. Dance is the only way I can really communicate how I feel and who I am. I'd like to perform the African dance I did when I auditioned for the Oakland Performing Arts Middle School. This is part of a dance by the Kikuyu people to celebrate a good hunt."

Jessie fast forwarded the tape to the number on her script. This music was pulsating and melodious. Addie Mae's movements, combined with the commanding African music, electrified the audience. She stomped, leaped, gestured, and swayed. Jessie saw several of the elderly people lift their hands in appreciation. As the last drumbeat drifted away, Addie Mae sank into a crouch, her head bowed. Again, applause thundered. One man pounded his cane.

This is going a lot better than we hoped. We are talented, thought Jessie.

"Our next Dreamgirl, Julie Stone, selected one of the oldest instruments in the world to master. In the face of enormous hardship, she has persevered."

Jessie moved the chair to the center. She carried Julie's violin and handed it to her after she was seated, the crutches by her side. Keeping Julie's part short had been deliberate. Julie wanted her violin to speak for her. The group had agreed.

"My name is Julie Stone. Like Mkiwa, I can't remember when I didn't want to play the violin. I take lessons on Saturday and practice every night. Whenever I play, I am happy. This is my favorite piece. I hope you like it."

There were moments when Julie's playing touched Jessie so deeply that she wanted to cry. Julie was oblivious to the audience. As her bow moved across the strings for the last time, Jessie saw a tear fall on her cheek. The silence in the audience lasted for several seconds. It ended with applause and shouts of "Brava!" Julie grinned. Addie Mae and Maria helped her move to the back.

Jessie exhaled. No one had made any mistakes. In fact, they had been at their best. *I just hope that I can do my part as well.*

"Now, I switch from narrator to performer. I am still Jessie Williams."

People chuckled.

Jessie continued. "My grandmother, Mamatoo, is the artistic director of a repertory theater company here in Oakland. I've been going to plays since I was born!

My dream is to become a famous dramatic actress. I realize that this will be difficult. Not many make it, and there are few parts for African-Americans, but I am determined. To audition for acceptance at the Oakland Performing Arts Middle School, I selected Sojourner Truth's speech, 'Ain't I a Woman?' It is my pleasure to share her powerful words with you."

Like the rest of her group, Jessie delivered a flawless performance. This time she was able to erase everyone before her. In moments she escaped back to 1851 and that packed hall. The words and intonations flowed like music. The audience's response startled her. Maria's mother was leading the cheers! Jessie was relieved that their work had been videotaped. Their stories plus the interviews with some of the residents about their lives would make a great project.

After two bows, Mrs. Winters explained that from now on the girls would be entertaining the residents twice a month. A table laden with punch, sandwiches, and cake stood in the corner. She invited everyone for refreshments. Before the girls could even change clothes, people came up to shake their hands and thank them.

Jessie watched an elderly black woman who walked with a cane beckon to Julie. The woman walked with a distinctive style, her eyes clear. The two of them sat down together. So Julie had already begun her interviews. Both Maria and Cooper were talking with certain residents.

For a second, the girls gazed at one another. An understanding passed between them. Going home depressed and dejected about the audition results would have been foolish and irresponsible. Coming here and performing was great.

After a half hour, Jessie gave the signal that it was time to leave. Only Julie remained, still engaged in animated conversation with the elderly black woman.

Jessie walked over to them.

"Those violin lessons my daughter took paid off. She's not a violinist in an orchestra or group, but she continues to play. Sandra enjoys her work as a real estate agent." The woman sipped her punch.

"The violin is the only thing that makes me happy now," said Julie.

"I can well imagine that. My son almost lost his home in that fire. He lived not that far from you. If that terrible wind hadn't shifted . . . No sense dwelling on that."

Julie stared hard at nothing. "The insurance company won't pay us what they should. And Daddy and Mom fight about whether or not to rebuild, Mrs. Lee. It's horrible at home, if you can call where we live home."

"It takes time to feel at home anywhere. I certainly don't feel as if this place is my home. Your parents are dealing with some very serious decisions, Julie. I lived with my son during that time, but after the fire I felt safer down here in the flatlands. He doesn't like this arrangement, but at least he has a dog and two cats to keep him company." Mrs. Lee chuckled.

"He likes animals?"

"Well, he never seemed too partial toward them. But after the fire, those three wandered into his life. No one ever claimed them. He doesn't have the heart to send them to the animal shelter."

Jessie interrupted. "Excuse me, please. Julie, we have to leave. Maria's mom is waiting to drive us home."

Julie shook Mrs. Lee's hand. "I'll be back, Mrs. Lee. Can we talk some more?"

"Of course. You and I have so much in common. Now, stop fretting so much, Julie. You're long overdue for a basket full of good luck to land in your lap."

"I hope so."

The girls retreated into the small room to change back into their school clothes. Deciding to dress for their parts had made a world of difference.

"I can't wait to come back here. Your mother's idea to work here was fantastic, Maria," said Julie, her eyes shining. "I love Mrs. Lee. I want to interview her."

Addie Mae zipped her skirt. "Dancing free and for the joy of it felt good. I think they really liked us."

Maria glowed. "Just wait until we come back. We're going to have to come up with something spectacular to top what we did today!"

Jessie nodded. "We can. Remember our motto."

The girls stopped. "Four, three, two, one. We're the best. Let's have some fun!"

As they left, Mrs. Lee thanked them for coming. Mrs. Winters was on the telephone. She put the caller on hold and added her appreciation. Mrs. Lee walked to the door with them.

"Now, Julie, don't you worry. Everything will work out. It just takes time," she called.

Addie Mae frowned. "What's that lady talking about?"

Jessie looked hard at nothing. After all, Julie had sworn her to secrecy.

"Nothing." Julie paused, balancing herself on the crutches.

"Then why would she say something like that?"

"Look, it's none of our business," said Maria.

"Cooper, you don't say much about your family. We've stopped hassling you. Maybe all of us have secrets," said Jessie. After all, she had promised Julie to keep her secret. *I have my own secret. I'd hate for anybody just to blab it out. Ugly words hurt.*

Mkiwa put her hands up. "Forget I asked anything!"

The door to the residence home opened. Mrs. Hernandez stuck her head out.

"Maria, here are the car keys. Girls, wait in the car for me. I have to talk to someone," she said.

The four girls arranged themselves in the car. Julie sat up front while Maria put the crutches in the back. Jessie and Addie Mae sorted themselves out in the back. Maria slid across the driver's side to sit next to Julie. The car was an older model without bucket seats. Everyone found someplace to plant her eyes. No one spoke.

"I don't understand what the big deal is," complained Addie Mae. "All I do is ask a simple question and suddenly I'm the enemy."

Silence.

"You're not the enemy," murmured Julie.

"Let's change the subject. What are we going to do for them in two weeks?" asked Jessie, trying to take the pressure off Julie.

"It's no good, Jessie, but thanks for trying. I'm tired of holding this in. Look, Cooper, my family got burned out in the fire in the hills last October. We owned a house near Jessie's. It caught fire. Everything we owned burned." Julie turned around. "And I mean everything. We had to run for our lives."

"I'm sorry, Julie. I didn't know," mumbled Mkiwa.

"How could you, Cooper? I know you three better than anybody else at OPA. You should know about what happened to me," said Julie.

Maria sighed. "I thought so, but I didn't know what to say."

Julie nodded. "I know. My parents are going nuts trying to decide what to do. We moved into this neighborhood because a friend of Daddy's said we could live here for almost nothing until things got better. But they haven't. Between the insurance company, my folks fighting, and my baby brother, this fall has been a disaster. Without OPA, my music, and the three of you, I couldn't have made it this far," Julie explained.

Jessie eyed Julie. Mrs. Stone, her mother, had been right. Julie Stone had a thread of steel in her back.

Maybe you can only hold a hurting thing in so long, she pondered.

"I'm so sorry I opened my big mouth. Two girls in my dance class had the same thing happen to them. One of them tried to go back and get her dog, but the house was burning so bad she couldn't." Addie Mae shook her head. "She talks about that dog constantly."

Jessie saw Julie's shoulders hunch together. Maria turned to her. Julie was crying.

"Oh, shoot! What did I say now?" said Addie Mae. "I'm keeping my mouth shut."

Through Julie's sobs, Jessie struggled to piece together what Julie was sharing.

"Daddy wouldn't let me go back for Toby. He . . . he said there wasn't enough time . . . and I had to leave Toby," sobbed Julie.

"You don't have to talk about it," soothed Maria.

Jessie spoke up, remembering how Julie had been acting during the past weeks. This wasn't the time to treat her like some fragile, brittle object. "Yes, Julie does. If she tells us, she'll feel better. Who's Toby?"

"My cat. I raised him since he was . . . born. I never found his body but he must have died in . . . the fire! I miss him!"

"You can get another cat," Addie Mae said.

"Sure, just like you keep getting new names? Come on, this is serious," Maria said.

"My life is serious, too!" said Addie Mae. "A name

is very important. I don't just pick names because it's fun to do! I have good reasons for what I do."

"Like what?" asked Jessie.

"Like maybe my life isn't so great. Maybe names help me try to figure out who I want to be. Get off me, Jessie." Mkiwa stared out the window.

"What a conversation! OK, Cooper, forget it. Now, come on, Julie," said Jessie, "you remember what Mrs. Lee told you about her son finding that dog and two cats. What if Toby didn't die in the fire?"

Julie turned around, her face wet with tears. "What do you mean?"

"It's a long shot, but maybe Toby got out. There were lots of stories in the newspaper about animals that escaped the fire," Jessie said.

"After all these months?" Addie Mae shook her head.

"We could ask people around where Julie lived. Put up a flyer with a drawing of Toby on it," Maria volunteered.

"Is there anything unusual about the way Toby looks or acts?" Addie Mae asked.

Julie thought. "Toby's a runt, the last of the litter. He never learned to run straight. He runs sideways and he has a scar on his back left leg that looks like a half moon."

"That's a lot. Who draws the best?" asked Jessie.

"I have one photograph," Julie said. "We can make copies of it."

"You can borrow one of my cats until we find yours."

"Thanks, Maria, but the only cat I want is Toby."

"Then we'll just have to get busy," said Jessie. "And find him."

"Or find out what happened to him," reminded Addie Mae.

Jessie spoke up. "Either way we'll find Toby."

The conversation ended.

That evening, Jessie sought sanctuary in her grandmother's apartment. Mamatoo bustled about. Outside, the rain poured. She had to tell Mamatoo about the results of the audition. But how?

Jessie blurted the truth out. "Mamatoo, I didn't get the part of Harriet as an old woman. I get to play Mary Ann, one of her sisters."

"How do you feel about that?" Mamatoo stopped and waited.

"Terrible. I really blew the audition! All that work and practice was for nothing! I messed up."

"You'll never be an actress with that attitude, Jessie. You got a part. Many who tried out didn't get anything. You learn how to audition by auditioning! If you want to make me proud of you, then be the best Mary Ann you can!"

Jessie stared at her grandmother.

"But Cass never failed like this. What's Dad going to say?"

"How are your grades?"

"Pretty good, I think."

"That's primarily what he cares about. As for your sister, stop comparing yourself to her. How did your friends do?"

"Just about as bad as me."

Mamatoo sighed. "Look on the bright side, Jess. You haven't mentioned your red hair in a while. Your face is cleared up. You have new friends. And—"

"I get your point. I need to be grateful for what I have. But auditioning for a part and not getting it is hard."

"Well, at least you're not alone. Now, help me clear this table. I've got to do some work on the play. The second act isn't going well," she said.

Jessie stacked the plates. Concerns poured through her mind just like the rain. *Where is Toby? What if he is dead? Can I ever do what Julie did? Tell my secret?*

chapter 8

By Friday, Julie had made photocopies of a picture of her missing cat, Toby. During Family Hour, the girls worked on drafting a flyer describing him. Addie Mae proved to be the most artistic of the group. She designed a flyer with a huge black caption that read, HELP US FIND TOBY.

Jessie watched her work. With firm, bold strokes, Addie Mae labored. It was evident that she was determined to make up for what she had said in the car.

Beneath the caption Addie Mae taped a copy of the photograph and neatly printed a description that included only the most important information. Julie's phone number was the next to last piece of information. Jessie watched as Addie Mae tapped the marking pen on the desk. Then she wrote, BRING A FIRE VICTIM HOME.

It was Maria who suggested everybody chipping in to run off a hundred copies of the flyer. Then Jessie had an idea.

"We can't do this alone. Why not make it a project for the whole class? I mean, if Mr. Reynolds is serious about this family stuff then he would support us," she said.

"Maybe Julie doesn't want everybody knowing her business," Addie Mae said, her voice tight.

"What if . . ." Julie looked off.

The group sat mute.

Maria spoke up. "If Toby is dead or we can't find him, then at least we tried, Julie. You won't have to go on keeping this to yourself wondering where he might be. If we do find him, it will be like finding a needle in a haystack."

Jessie butted in. "But there are a lot of miracles connected with the fire. The newspaper still has stories about found pets and families who are getting unexpected help. It's not like the fire is over and forgotten. All you have to do is to look up at the hills and see what the fire did."

"What's going on here, Fours?" Mr. Reynolds stood next to them. His eyes swept over the draft of the flyer. "Miss Cooper, are you also an artist?" The group clammed up.

"Mr. Reynolds, we need a few minutes to talk privately about something. OK?" asked Jessie.

"Sure." He moved to another cluster.

"Julie, it's up to you. We can try to do this ourselves or get the rest of the class to help," said Jessie.

Addie Mae shifted in her seat. "I want to say something. Those girls I told you about in my dance class, the ones that got burned out, well, they are just like you, Julie. Sad. Lonely. The only reason I found out about what happened to them is because I was talking about my father and mentioned that he was an Oakland fireman."

"We know. A lot of firemen got hurt," exclaimed Julie.

Addie Mae sighed. "Yes. He almost died in that fire. Anyway, there must be more kids like you. This could help a lot of people."

Julie's brow wrinkled. "I don't understand, Cooper."

"I haven't thought it all the way through. But if that happened to me, maybe I'd like to know there was someplace to go to where I could at least listen to other kids like me. It's hard to keep secrets about things that tear you up. That's all I have to say."

"So if I tell the class and they help, that increases my chances of finding out one way or the other?" Julie was talking to herself. "It's nothing to be ashamed of. I mean, you didn't make fun of me or make me feel bad. All right, let's try it. Thanks, Cooper."

Jessie raised her hand. "Mr. Reynolds, we need you."

Five minutes later, their teacher smiled. "I never know what to expect from the Fours. You constantly surprise me. I think your idea has merit, but I don't want you to put all of your hopes on finding Toby. Remember that trying together is what counts in the long run. It's time to tell the class.''

The four girls stood in front of the class. Addie Mae nudged Julie forward. In halting tones, Julie explained her situation and what she needed the class to do. To their surprise they got instant approval. In fact, three of their classmates had been burned out in the fire. Two others had come close to it.

Jessie thought about what Addie Mae had said. Perhaps some kind of support group would be a good idea. But right now there was too much to do. Discovering what happened to Toby was near the top of her list.

On the way to their humanities core, the girls plotted. There was a copy place two blocks away. During lunchtime, with Mr. Reynolds's permission, they used the school copier to make enough copies of the flyer to post around school.

There would be plenty to pass out to their Family Hour class, to staple in stores and onto telephone poles over the weekend. Then it was a question of waiting. Julie had already contacted the animal shelters. But there hadn't been any leads about a cat that fit Toby's description.

Reluctantly, Jessie entered the theater for the last session of the improv class. She sat in the back by herself. Miss Baker was announcing another reader's theater audition the following week. The performance would be held the week of October 26.

Intrigued by the uniqueness of the story, Jessie paid close attention. The script had been written using the book *Lon Po Po*, a Red Riding Hood story from China by an author and illustrator named Ed Young. There would be six roles: the narrator; the good mother; Shang, the eldest daughter; Tao, the middle daughter; Paotze, the youngest daughter; and Lon Po Po, Granny Wolf.

The story was thought to be over a thousand years old. Jessie leaned forward as Miss Baker explained it. One day, when the mother left to visit the girls' grandmother, a wolf came to the door.

The wolf, Lon Po Po, lied to the sisters. Pretending to be their cold and tired grandmother, the wolf weaseled his way into the house. Jessie marveled at the sisters' cleverness in tricking and finally killing the wolf.

I like this story. What if I tried out for the role of the oldest sister? She's the smartest. Mamatoo said I have to keep trying out, no matter what, thought Jessie. *I don't know. I have to work on the yucky part of Mary Ann, Harriet Tubman's little sister; help Julie; get ready for the next performance at Evergreen, and do my schoolwork. Maybe I should pass on this one.*

Then Jessie thought about that small red autumn tree she had seen by the road. Eventually the winter winds and rains would strip it of every leaf, but in time, the leaves would return. For now, that little tree wasn't giving up or giving in. *Why not try out for that part? What do I have to lose?*

The class concluded with a review of the major im-

provisation techniques and exercises they had practiced. River, Sylvia, and some of the other older students demonstrated advanced improvisation exercises.
As usual, their skill made Jessie gasp. She heard the
theater door open behind her. Jamar.

"Hi. You feeling better, Red?" he teased, dropping
his book bag on the floor.

"Jamar, it takes enormous effort to forget that on top
of my head, I am wearing a burning bush. Don't force
me to remember," whispered Jessie. "No, I don't feel
better. I got a nothing part."

"Sorry."

"Forget it. This is a bad day for me. A bad week. My
hair still bothers me. I mean, the allergy rash is gone,
but sometimes I wish I was . . ."

Jamar stared at her. "Was what? I like the way you
look, Jessie. You've got your own style. I like that."

A hot flush swept over her face.

"Can we be . . . friends?" he asked.

Jessie swallowed. "I thought we were."

"We are. But I wanted you to know that I think
you're special." He looked at her. "Special to me, I
mean."

"Special? Me? That's something I have to think
about, Jamar," Jessie said.

"That's what I like about you, Jessie. You think
about what you are going to do, first. Most kids don't."

Jessie laughed. "Not as much as I should. Look at
my hair!"

Friday Family Hour went well. The flyers were

posted around school. Classmates offered to put them up in their neighborhoods. Each of the girls separated to go to her individual practice for the Winter Festival.

Just as Jessie had expected, she was assigned to scenery construction and painting in addition to her part. The rehearsal schedule was grueling. In a way, Jessie was relieved that she hadn't won the more complex part she had sought. Then it all would have been much harder.

Before she ran to catch the bus, she stopped off at the school library and checked out a copy of the script for the upcoming reader's theater production of *Lon Po Po*. She had one short weekend to do her schoolwork, prepare for the audition, and staple Julie's flyers. By the time Jessie opened the front door, she was tired.

"Jessie, is that you?" called Mrs. Williams.

"Mom, why are you home so early?"

"I got a call from school about Cass. She's been cutting classes. Do you have any idea what might be going on with her?" Jessie's mother paced back and forth.

Jessie's stomach plummeted. Joe. Cass and Joe. What was Cass up to? She'd promised to keep her sister's secret. She'd promised to be Cass's friend. No matter what. A promise was a promise.

"I don't know, Mom. You'll have to talk to her. Cass must have a good reason," said Jessie, fleeing downstairs. "I've got mountains of homework to do."

An hour later, Jessie stretched. She turned the com-

Chapter Eight

163

puter screen off. The first draft of her paper on life in ancient Egypt was completed. When she heard her grandmother's car, she ran down the hall, waited, then pressed the buzzer. One long, three short.

Tonight Mamatoo was wrapped in a long red wool shawl. Weary eyes greeted Jessie. Her grandmother nodded and went into her bedroom. Jessie knew what that greeting meant. Mamatoo's right hand was trembling more than usual.

Parkinson's disease scared Jessie. Mamatoo refused to cut back on her theater work. *Nobody* told her grandmother what to do. Jessie bustled about. She put the teakettle on. Next, she opened the refrigerator and took out the fixings for a salad. Then, she put a bowl of cold vegetable pasta on the counter. After Jessie finished the salad, she cut the French bread into slices, buttered them, and arranged them under the small broiler.

Setting the table by the sliding glass doors took only minutes. Mamatoo loved her black-and-red striped stoneware dishes. Jessie admired a vase of mixed fall flowers. When the teakettle whistled, she quickly grabbed a teapot shaped like a pyramid and filled it with hot tap water.

After she placed the food on the table, she emptied the warm teapot, filled it with the boiling hot water from the kettle, and added two tea bags. She went over to the stereo set and turned to the radio station she knew her grandmother liked. Knowing how candlelight soothed her grandmother, Jessie hurried to light the tall ivory candles. She admired the stunning effect.

"Oh, Jessie!" Mamatoo emerged from her bedroom in her red velour robe and slippers. "What a blessing you are! How did you know I was too exhausted to fix anything to eat?"

Jessie beamed. She pulled one of the dining room chairs out. With a slight curtsey, Mamatoo took a seat. Jessie joined her.

They ate a peaceful dinner. Jessie cleared the table and set a plate of fruit and more tea on a lacquer tray. While Mamatoo relaxed in her favorite chair, Jessie made a fire and covered her grandmother with a woolen throw.

"I can't tell you how happy you've made me this evening. I decided not to go back to the theater to-night. Just too tired," sighed Mamatoo. "My, I was hungrier than I thought. I feel so much better, honey."

Jessie handed her a cup of tea. She snuggled back on the sofa and enjoyed the crackling fire. The safe feeling in the small apartment was one she relished. Here the only expectation she had to meet was to be herself. Even if that meant being a bold redheaded girl with roller-coaster emotions.

"Now, catch me up on your life."

"I'll be building and painting scenery for the Winter Festival play," grimaced Jessie. "But I have decided to go for a part in the next reader's theater perform-ance."

Mamatoo sipped her tea. "Admirable. That's what a real actress does. Stay vigilant and hone your craft. That separates you from the ones who don't have enough heart to struggle for their dreams."

Jessie told her about Julie and Toby. Mamatoo offered to take flyers to her theater company. They chatted on. The buzzer sounded. No code, just abrupt pulses.

"Now, who in the world is making all of that racket?"

Jessie leaped up. "You stay put. I'll get it."

She opened the door to see Cass sobbing before her. Class flew in and flopped on the couch, clutching a pillow to her tearstained face.

"Do I live in Grand Central Station? Sometimes I think I'd have more privacy in a public restroom," Mamatoo said.

Cass sobbed on. The buzzer sounded again. One long.

"We know who that is," said Jessie.

Mom strode in like a military marching band. She headed straight for Cass.

"Why not sell admission tickets, since my apartment has become a family theater? Then I could find a refuge in a foreign country and dwell in solitude far away from the vicissitudes of the Williams family life."

"Mother, don't you see that we have a problem? Haven't I been a good parent? Don't I deserve daughters who tell me the truth?" said Mrs. Williams, hands

on both hips. "Cass, I am stunned. Your behavior de-
fies description! You have never done anything to
upset this family. And now this. I don't know what to
think."

Cass continued to weep.

Jessie's mind spun. What could be going on? If Cass
had gotten into some kind of trouble with Joe . . . Jess
slammed that door. No way.

"Daughter, sit down. Jessie, pour your distraught
mother a cup of tea and your hysterical sister a glass of
juice. Is my son-in-law home yet?" Mamatoo asked,
shifting under the blanket.

"No, he's got two authors reading tonight so he
won't be home until later."

"Be grateful for that, daughter. I hate to referee
family interactions. At my age I should be allowed
to simply sit and be a member of the audience
of life, not a participant. But since you two have dis-
turbed my tranquillity, one that, I might add, Jessie
worked very hard to create for me, let the games
begin." Mamatoo leaned back and folded her hands
together.

Jessie perched on the arm of her grandmother's
chair.

"Mother, did you know that Cassandra has missed
the past three days of school? Did you know that today
I got a call at work from her school counselor asking if
she was ill? She refuses to tell me where she has been
and with whom."

"I haven't been anywhere, Mom. I just needed some time to think." Cass wiped at her eyes. "Alone."

"What in the world do you need to think about? Aren't you doing great in school? Didn't you make the cheerleading squad? Don't you have your choice of colleges to attend? Haven't you and Joe settled your problems?" retorted her mother.

"Perhaps that is why the child needs some time alone," said Mamatoo.

"Oh, Mother, there you go again, being enigmatic. Cutting three days of classes is serious. Cassandra, are you in some kind of trouble?"

Jessie fought back a gasp. That was the same question that was troubling her. She prayed.

"No, Mom. I'm not pregnant."

"Well, *that* never occurred to me. We've discussed sex. We agreed that you are much too young for any serious intimate involvement, Cass. You have your whole life ahead of you. I know that you and Joe are in love, but we fall in love many times," said her mother.

Mamatoo spoke up. "Daughter, since you saw fit to bring this drama into my living room, may I speak? Cassandra, think long and hard about whether you want your life to completely change. I don't believe that you do, no matter how much he is pressuring you."

Shocked, Jessie felt her eyes widen.

"Mamatoo, how did you know Joe was giving me a hard time about that?" asked Cass in surprise.

Mamatoo chuckled. "Once upon a time I was your age and in love and a boy did everything he could, including dating another girl, to manipulate me into going to bed with him. I cut school for two weeks. To think. Just to get my mind together."

"Where did you go?" asked Jessie.

"To the movies or the library or just wandered around. Each day I came back home and pretended that I had gone to school. Eventually my parents found out. I was grounded for six months. That solved part of my dilemma, but not my broken heart. A new boyfriend finally healed that."

Jessie looked at her sister. This was not the self-assured, perfect sibling she had judged herself against throughout the years. It was startling to see confident, unflappable Cass miserable and confused. And it was deeply unsettling, too.

"I should leave. I mean, this is Cass's private business." Jessie stood up.

"No, stay, Jessie," Cass said. "I need you. Please."

Right then, Jessie's heart filled with love for her sister. Tears welled in her eyes. She knew that Cass meant each and every word. They weren't just blood sisters. They were becoming buddies.

"Jess, what do you know about this?" Mrs. Williams's voice was loud.

"Mom, what Cass shared with me is between me and her. We have the right to know things about each other and keep them private," replied Jessie.

"No, you don't! Especially not when your sister is in trouble."

Jess held firm. "Mom, I don't want to be disrespect-ful, but Cass is my sister, first. If she wants anybody to know anything, that's her decision to tell, not mine."

"Jessie, don't you understand that there are times when keeping secrets can hurt the person you love more than it will ever help them?" asked Mamatoo. "You have to think very carefully now. Is this one of those times?"

"That's not my answer to give." Jessie stared at Cass.

"What is disturbing you so deeply, Cass?" asked her grandmother.

"Joe is dating another girl to make me jealous. All of a sudden he started changing. At first I thought that everything was great between us. But then he started pushing us going to the same college and getting en-gaged in June and—"

Mrs. Williams jumped up, and the cup tumbled to the floor. "And getting engaged? Have you lost your mind? You haven't even graduated from high school! My heavens! What has been going on with you? Have I been this blind?"

Mamatoo spoke up, her words spaced for emphasis. "Daughter, listen to your child. Sometimes, we miss the forest for the trees. I think that Cassandra is attempting to share something that is extremely diffi-cult."

As Jess listened she thought about Cass telling her that people expected her to be perfect. How they saw only what they wanted to see, never the real person Cass was beneath the light skin, straight hair, light eyes, and sparkling personality. Her sister was right.

Jessie remembered the vow she had made to Cass. The promise to be her friend. She looked to Mamatoo, but the elderly woman was watching Cass.

"Mom, Cass has the right to be mixed-up. She's not perfect."

"Is this some kind of conspiracy? Jessie, what in the world do you know about any of this? You're much too young!"

"No, I'm not. I've never had a boyfriend, but it must be hard. There's this boy at school who likes me and wants to be my friend. Just knowing that makes my stomach ache. I'm not even ready to think about going out on a date with him or any boy! Imagine how Cass feels," argued Jessie passionately.

"The child has a point, daughter. Cassandra is in love. I can recall a time when you were sprawled on the floor in your bedroom wailing and moaning just like Cassandra. What was that boy's name?" Mamatoo fluttered her fingers as if she was trying to lure a name out of the air.

"Mother, this is not the time to digress into the past."

"I beg to disagree with you, daughter. Especially when the past is repeating itself before your very eyes. Sam . . . Samuel. That was his name! Samuel!"

"Mom, it was Dad!" exclaimed both sisters.

Mrs. Williams bent over and picked up the teacup. As she walked to the kitchen to get a paper towel, she turned and flung her mother a look that would topple a skyscraper. After pouring herself another cup of tea and sitting in a far chair, she spoke.

"Mother, one day I will get you for pulling that one on me. You have made your point. Cass, is this about Joe pressuring you to . . ." She couldn't finish.

Cass nodded her head. Jessie gulped, relieved that her worst fears were unfounded.

"Then you have to decide what you're going to do."

"I know what I'm going to do, Mom. I'm not ready to get serious and do what Joe wants. I'm still a kid. But I don't want to lose Joe. What did you do, Mom?" asked Cass.

Every eye fixed on Mrs. Williams.

"Excellent question, Cassandra," murmured Mama-too.

"I told your father that as much as I loved and wanted him, I was not ready. I told him that I wanted us to have more time together as friends without all of the emotions and complications that came with sex. And that for me, sex and marriage go together."

"What did he say?" asked Jessie.

"He broke up with me and dated other girls."

"Mom! Our father did that?"

Mamatoo snorted. "Think about me, not your mother! My life was purgatory for seven months! I dreaded coming home from work to this daughter of mine, sobbing, emptying crates of Kleenex, and declaring that she'd never smile again."

"Mother, I wasn't that bad!"

"No, you were worse!"

For the first time, everyone relaxed. The shared laughter lowered the temperature in the room to a tolerable level.

Cass said, "Joe told me he couldn't wait for years."

Jessie asked, "Mom, how did you and Dad get back together?"

Her mother shrugged her shoulders. "I started dating other fellows. Your grandmother made me. I didn't stop loving your father, but I did start liking myself more. I decided that we could never have anything lasting if I gave in to him because I was afraid of losing him. Keeping me was more important than losing him."

"That was one of the proudest times in my life, daughter. I knew that silly boy would come back. But I wasn't sure if you'd take him back," said Mamatoo.

"What about Cass?" asked Jessie.

"Does Dad have to know about this?"

"No, Cass. Let's keep this between the four of us."

"Thanks, Mom. I need time." Cassandra picked at the pattern on the sofa.

"We'll be here for you, Cass," said her mother, coming over and hugging her.

"Good. Let's move on to the next order of business. Now, Jess, who's this boy who wants to be your friend?" asked Mamatoo.

Jessie wanted to crawl under the couch. When her sister started to giggle, everyone joined in. After another forty minutes, Jess followed her sister to their bedroom.

Cass hugged her. Another crack splintered the wall inside of Jessie. But the wall still held the secret. As long as the wall stood, the secret lived. Jessie knew that, but what she had heard Mrs. Grant, the same Mrs. Grant everyone else thought was so great, say made her feel ashamed. What would her family think?

Over the weekend, Jessie stapled and passed out flyers for Julie. The part of Mary Ann in the Harriet Tubman play required minimal rehearsal. Reading for the oldest sister in the Chinese version of the Little Red Riding Hood story appealed to her more and more.

On Saturday, she and Cass went to the movies. It was fun. Jess wore her gold hoops. By Sunday night, she was prepared for another long week at the Oakland Performing Arts Middle School. Cass acted calmer. Joe called three times, but Cass only talked to him for a few minutes.

During the night, Jessie kept a vigil over her restless sister. If this was what falling in love was like, she didn't want it. Jamar would stay a friend forever.

Cass groaned in her sleep. Jessie wished that she could help her sister. Silently, she prayed that everything would turn out right. But as Mamatoo said, "Prayers need a boost." Jessie drifted off, wondering what boost she needed to fix some serious parts of her life.

chapter 9

On Thursday morning when Maria entered Home Base, her eyes were shining. Jessie yawned. Between the tension at home and her schedule at school, sleep wasn't enough. Addie Mae looked pooped. Not even her "Black and Proud of It" sweatshirt seemed to help. Julie seemed down. Jessie wondered if trying to find Toby had been a smart idea.

"Julie, did you go to any of the fire first-year anniversary events on Sunday?" asked Jessie.

She nodded. "My parents wanted to. We met people who are going to help us deal with the insurance company. And Dad talked to a neighbor of ours who bought his new house in a kit! Can you imagine that? So it didn't take him long to get a new house up. Now my folks are talking to each other more than yelling at each other."

"I'm glad you went," said Jessie. "Do you get the *Phoenix Journal*? That newspaper that helps fire survivors? It's great."

"Not as often as we should."

"Well, we do. I'll bring you copies each time it comes out. And I know you can get back copies. My dad has all of them. There's tons of information about rebuilding, money, and even a series about two cats who are trying to get home," shared Jessie.

"Thanks."

"No big deal." But the smile on Julie's face told Jessie it was.

"Hey! Look what my mother brought home last night!" exclaimed Maria, waving a brown envelope.

Three sets of weary eyes waited.

"These are thank-you letters from the people at Evergreen! They loved us. They can't wait until we visit again next Monday."

"We haven't even planned what we're going to do for them," Addie Mae groaned.

"We will. We always do," said Jessie. "After all, how can we exist until the end of our first semester, unless we keep thinking on our feet?"

"Just read these!" Maria handed letters around.

Mr. Reynolds was taking roll.

"Miss Williams?" he asked, lifting his head.

"Right here."

"Miss Hernandez?"

"Here."

"Miss Stone, how is your ankle?"

"Much better, thank you."

"Any news on Toby?"

Her face dropped. "No, not a word."

"Keep trying. And Miss Cooper?"

Every day Jessie hoped that Addie Mae would just use her own name.

"Present." Addie Mae's voice was strident.

While he continued taking roll, the girls read the letters. They were wonderful. Jessie admired the elegant writing and stationery. She was amazed at how much detail was in each letter. Julie grinned.

"Mrs. Lee said that she is looking forward to seeing us on Monday! She wrote a special little note at the end of the letter to me!"

"Let's meet at lunch and plan what we'll do. Why not a simple recital using what we're working on for the Winter Festival," said Jessie.

"Sounds like a plan to me," said Addie Mae.

Everyone agreed.

The days blurred for Jessie. Get up. Get dressed. Get the bus. Get exhausted at school. Get home. Get more exhausted by homework. Get busy practicing the part of Mary Ann. Get serious about the reader's theater audition. Get to bed. Get up. And then the whole routine repeated itself.

By the end of the day Friday, Jessie had to will herself to walk into the theater. She had to audition for reader's theater today. The gold hoop earrings shone. The part of Shang, the oldest daughter in *Lon Po Po*, could end up being her first part as a young person. Not many students were there. She saw Jamar. Her stomach flip-flopped.

He sat down next to her. Jessie squirmed.

"Hi."

"Hi. Are you trying out for a part, Jamar?"

He smiled. "Nope. I just hoped you might show up. Look, Jess, I've got years ahead of me to go to school, work, learn politics. I'll have to start at the bottom and work up, step by step. So what? That'll make me a much stronger and smarter senator."

Jessie frowned. "I guess there's a message for me in that?"

"What are friends for? Sure there is."

"I got it. The same is true for me about becoming a good actress," laughed Jessie. "Step by step."

"Right! You going to the Halloween dance?" he asked.

"I haven't thought about it much. I can't get caught up," Jessie admitted.

Jamar's face fell. "Try to come. Let me know. Can I have your phone number? Here's mine." He handed her a slip of paper.

Too taken aback to think, Jessie recited her phone number. Jamar wrote it down. She placed his slip of paper in her purse. *I never had a boy call me! Wow!*

Mr. Reynolds's voice boomed through the room. "Tryouts for the part of Shang, stage front, now."

Four girls got up. Jessie read last.

"Good job, Miss Williams," said Mr. Reynolds.

Jessie started to walk off the stage.

"Just a minute. I'd like you to read the part of Lon Po Po, Granny Wolf. Start on the first page. Remember this is a wolf pretending to be an old woman," he said, taking a seat.

Jamar had moved closer to the front. He gave her the thumbs-up sign. With shaky hands, Jessie held the script. She turned to the first page. Granny Wolf was the big part. But not exactly the one she wanted. Jessie exhaled. If persistent effort was what counted, she'd give this her best try.

As she started to read, the magic of the theater carried Jessie away from the small OPA theater. She was in China, a China that had existed over a thousand years ago. What a crafty, manipulative, dangerous creature she was! A wolf disguised as the grandmother of three precious little girls. A wolf up to no good. Such a wicked wolf doomed to a justly gruesome fate. When Jess finished reading, she shook her head as if to clear it.

Jamar clapped.

Mr. Reynolds smiled. "Now that's what I call a fine reading! The results will be posted Monday."

Jessie Williams left the stage, delighted to hear such rare praise from Mr. Reynolds. Was it possible that she'd be playing another old woman? This time a wolf in disguise? Inside, she laughed. A redheaded African-American girl playing a wolf pretending to be an elderly Chinese grandmother? At OPA anything could happen! One look at Jamar's face persuaded her that it was a possibility.

Jessie and Jamar walked to the bus stop together. He waited with her until the bus came. Jessie waved to him. Having Jamar as a friend might just work out.

Once home, Jess was surprised to see her father's car. Dad never took a day off or came home early. Puzzled, she opened the front door. There he stood on the deck.

"Hi, Dad."

Her father turned around.

"Jessie. How was school?"

She let her book bag fall and flung her jacket on the coatrack. Dad looked tired.

"I ended up trying out for another old woman role. I was good, Dad. It's the biggest part in the script."

He frowned. "Jessie, what about your academic subjects? Aren't grades due soon?"

"Dad, acting is an academic subject. Yes, grades come in tomorrow. I'm not worried about any of them. I've been studying hard. I don't plan to get anything below a B or B+," she said.

"Jess, what is going on here at home? No one talks to me. Not your mother or Mamatoo. Cassandra avoids me like the plague. Do you know what's going on, Jessie?"

Jessie's shoulders sagged. One more secret to keep. If Mom wasn't talking then there was no way she would. *If Mom isn't talking, I'm keeping my mouth shut. Where was Mom? Mamatoo? Cass? Anybody?* Her father's eyes were boring in on her like a drill.

"Look, Dad, like you always say, Mom knows everything that's going on," said Jessie.

He squinted at her. "Jessie, that is one of the best non-answers to a question I have ever heard. I'll rephrase my question: Do you have any personal knowledge of something unusual going on in this family that involves your sister?"

Shifting from foot to foot, Jessie almost jumped out of her skin when the telephone rang. She ran for the telephone. It was Addie Mae.

"Hi, Cooper. Thanks for calling. Thanks a lot," she said.

"Sounds like this phone call came at a good time. No, don't tell me. I've gotten in enough trouble asking questions."

Jessie took a deep breath. "What's up?"

"You know next week is special? Remember we have to do all that different dressing up every day?"

Jessie had forgotten. A bulletin had been posted. In the week before Halloween, each day was a dress event. Monday was Crazy Day, where everyone wore mixed and unmatched weird clothes. Tuesday was Opposites Day. Girls dressed like boys and boys dressed like girls. GQ Day on Wednesday meant getting all decked out and looking good.

Thursday would be easy—School Colors Day. And

finally on Friday there was Costumes Day, with a parade and judging for the best, most creative, and funniest costume. They also had to present to the senior citizens on Monday after school. If she got selected for the reader's theater performance, she'd have to practice and then perform on Thursday and Friday. Next week would be a nightmare.

"I forgot about that. Thanks for reminding me. What else is up?"

"I don't know what to do. I have to practice hard for the Winter Festival. I have to make the second line of dancers. And there are problems at home. Jessie, I don't want the others to think that I don't want to be a part of Crazy Week," said Addie Mae, "but I just can't get organized for it and concentrate on my dancing."

Jessie changed the phone to her other ear. "You don't have to get dressed up. Nobody will care, Cooper. Like Maria said, everybody has problems at home."

"Not like the ones I have. Look, I know the kids think I'm strange because I changed my name twice, but they don't understand. Nobody does. I've got to go. My father is taking my mother and me out to dinner tonight and to see a movie. We always have a lot of fun together. I shouldn't have bothered you. Sorry."

"Wait, Cooper! Don't hang up. I thought you just said you had some serious problems at home," said Jessie.

"It's all mixed up. My father puts his family first. We

go on vacations three or four times a year and every week we go out to dinner and the show. It's like a family tradition. He likes those." She rattled on and on.

Jessie was getting tired of Addie Mae's ramblings about her unbelievable father. That was what her father was—unbelievable. In the two months they had known each other, not one person in the Fours had met or talked with this invincible but invisible father. According to Addie Mae, his schedule at the firehouse kept him away.

"Cooper, I know what your real name means."

"So?"

"I checked my African-American history. You were named after Addie Mae Collins, one of the four girls murdered in Birmingham, Alabama, in church on Sunday. I wouldn't be ashamed to have her name," said Jessie.

Addie Mae's voice was hushed. "I'm not ashamed, Jessie. It doesn't have anything to do with that."

Jessie protested, "But, Cooper, I saw pictures of the four girls in a magazine my father gave me. I saw a picture of Addie Mae Collins. She was just a kid, a sweet, pretty little girl. She looked like she was ten or eleven years old! She was a kid! Like us! Cooper, this isn't like Harriet Tubman or Sojourner Truth. They lived years and years ago. Addie Mae Collins would have been close to forty now. Are her parents alive? Do you know them? Have you ever been to Birmingham, Alabama?"

"Jessie, I don't want to talk about this. I can't and I can't explain it to you. You'd never understand. I have to go. Forget about my calling you," said Addie Mae.

"Wait a minute! You don't know me well enough to decide what I can understand. And that doesn't mean I want to know any more. Well, I do, but I'll stop. If somebody tells me another secret, I'm going to scream," said Jessie. "You're my size. Look, I'll bring some stuff next week that you can throw on. Nothing fancy, just enough so you don't feel weird."

"You don't have to do that. I wasn't calling asking for any help."

"You know what, Cooper, you turn even doing one little thing for you into a big deal. I know I don't have to. Maybe I'll need to change my name sometime and you can help me find a good one," teased Jessie.

"I know some great names that would fit you!" Addie Mae retorted.

Jessie laughed. "I bet you do." As she hung up, she shook her head. Mr. Reynolds was right. Her group was full of surprises.

By the time Cass ran in the door, her cheeks red, Dad had gone to work in his study. Jessie was setting the table for dinner. She had made a salad and taken out a container of frozen chili.

The telephone rang. Jessie rushed to pick it up. It was Joe. Jess didn't understand everything that was going on between her sister and Joe. But Joe was making her sister miserable.

"No, Joe, you can't talk to Cass. I'll tell her you called. Don't hang up on me. I want you to stop making my sister cry. No, don't call me a kid. I'm smart enough to know that what you're doing is wrong. If you really cared about Cass, you'd stop being mean to her. If you don't stop hassling her, you'll be sorry." Jessie slammed the telephone down.

"Jessie, do you realize what you just said to Joe?" Cass whispered. "I thought you liked him."

Jessie's heart jumped. "Oh, Cass, I hope you're not mad at me. He deserves to be told off."

"I'm not mad at you. You're so grown-up, Jess, you can stand up for me anytime!"

"You're my sister . . ." Jessie paused, "and my friend. I just want you to know that you're not alone."

Cass kissed her cheek. "I won't forget this. Where's Dad? I saw his van outside."

"He's in the study."

Cass silently tiptoed past the closed door and hurried downstairs. Jessie knew that she would barricade herself in the bathroom until Mom came home. Mom could handle anything, even a nosy Dad.

Getting ready for Crazy Day was a breeze. Jessie closed her eyes and reached for whatever she could. The result was a pink cotton dress with puffed sleeves, her old blue jeans, a red cardigan sweater, and her gym shoes. At the last minute she remembered her promise to Addie Mae and pulled out a wild polka-dot blouse and plaid skirt.

Bright and early on Monday morning, Jessie ran to the theater door in the far wing. She searched for the part of Shang, but her name was not after it. Jessie's eyes moved up a bit. There was her name. Jessie Williams had been selected to play the part of Lon Po Po, Granny Wolf, the lead part. *But what a lead!* Rehearsals would be held each lunch period and after school on Tuesday and Wednesday.

During Family Hour, the girls reviewed their program for the seniors that afternoon. Addie Mae smiled when Jessie handed her the clothes. Even Julie had dressed for the occasion.

"Where in the world did you get that great outfit?" Addie Mae asked. Then she clapped a hand over her mouth. "Sorry, forget the question!"

"I had more fun putting this together. When we lost our clothes in the fire, we didn't have much money for new clothes. I got some clothes from relatives and thrift shops," explained Julie. "There are lots of places with free clothes for fire survivors."

Julie wore a brand-new pair of red boots with a long, bright green peasant skirt with contrasting horizontal stripes of brown and gold. Black suspenders over a gold short-sleeved sweater with a white feather boa topped the outfit.

"As far as I'm concerned you win first prize!" Addie Mae said. The other girls agreed. Julie giggled.

Going through the day surrounded by weird kids started the week off with a bang. The experience of having performed in reader's theater before proved to be a blessing. Noon practice was easier. As difficult as it was for Jessie to admit, she really made a great wolf.

Again, the props would be simple—a tape of Chinese music and a simple backdrop copied from one of the illustrations. On each character's stand stood one symbol from the story, a candle, a basket, or a piece of strong rope. This time they would each wear a red T-shirt with black pants.

Practice ended. Jessie managed to gulp down half a cheese sandwich and run to her next class. Family Hour arrived. Jessie could tell that Julie had expected to learn something about Toby by now. There had been only one lead and the cat turned out to be a female Siamese. Not Toby.

Mr. Reynolds passed out their grades. Jessie reached for hers with confidence. Quickly, she skimmed the piece of paper. The B– in science/mathematics core stunned her. She hadn't thought that one test counted so much. Dad wouldn't like that.

Her only A was in improvisation and reader's theater. Dad would like that even less. She read the comments written by her teachers. They were encouraging, but nothing like what Cass got.

Addie Mae looked happy. But Maria didn't. Julie stuck the envelope in her book bag. No one spoke much on the way to Evergreen Residential Manor. Julie was very adept at using the crutches. They changed in the same small room.

This time Jessie began by thanking everyone for their wonderful letters. She explained that they would like a list of requests so they could plan programs around what their audience preferred. This time they would perform their favorite pieces.

At the end, an idea hit Jessie. She excused herself for a minute and returned with flyers in one hand. The girls stared at her. Mrs. Winters stood in the back, while Mrs. Hernandez waited to start videotaping.

"The four of us have a difficult problem. Everyone thinks that we are wasting our time. Maybe we are, but like our teacher Mr. Reynolds says, we have to try together," she said.

Around her she saw attentive, kind faces. Jessie felt as if she were surrounded by family.

"Julie Stone and her family were burned out in the horrible fire last fall. They lost everything," explained Jessie. "Julie lost her cat, Toby. I know that Mrs. Hernandez has passed around our flyers, but we want you to know how important this is. Toby is a male cat, who runs sideways and has a half-moon scar on his back left leg. He's just a regular cat, mostly gray with white paws. Here are more flyers. We'd appreciate it if you would ask your friends and relatives if they have seen Toby."

After the program, they devoted time to interviewing individual seniors. Julie and Mrs. Lee huddled together in a corner. Maria and Addie Mae both had friends to talk with. Jessie stared out the window. In a few hours she'd have to face her father with her grades.

"That was smart of you, Jessie," said Mrs. Hernandez, packing the camera.

"I keep hoping something happens. Even if we don't find Toby, Julie has to be convinced that we tried as hard as we could," said Jessie.

"You know, at first Maria's father and I were very worried about her attending OPA. Her father isn't pleased with Maria's desire to be a concert pianist. But he's willing to go along with this as—"

Jessie smiled. "—as long as she gets good grades and stays out of trouble."

"So your father is like Maria's," said Mrs. Hernandez.

As they left, a serious-looking African-American man came in, carrying a bouquet of yellow roses. He was dressed like a businessman. Jessie saw him head for the dayroom. Curious, she hung back a minute. Mrs. Lee's face broke into a huge grin as soon as she saw him. They embraced.

That must be Mrs. Lee's son, Jessie realized.

At home, dinner was a disaster. Dad made it clear that nothing below a B would be tolerated, and if there wasn't an A in something besides acting, she was on her way to Milton Middle School. Cass had her usual top grades. But Jessie didn't feel jealous. Nothing Dad said brought a smile to Cass's face. Joe called, but Cass refused to talk with him. Mom acted as if life was normal.

In the bedroom, Cass pounded away on the computer. Jessie couldn't figure out what to wear for Opposites Day, plus she had to bring something for Addie Mae. Maybe Dad would lend her his hat or tie.

"You can dress like a hobo," said Cass. "I'll help you. I think your grades are great for your first few months in middle school."

"Dad doesn't. I'd die if he made me leave OPA."

"You've gotten through the hardest part. Trust me, school gets easier after this."

"Except for boys."

Cass smiled. "Right. You told Joe off better than anybody could. I bet he's still holding the receiver with his mouth open! You got anybody you want me to tell off?"

The question caught Jess by surprise. "Yeah, Mrs. Grant. Tell her I'm not dumb and dull and ugly." The sentence came out in short, explosive bursts.

"Jess, what are you talking about?"

Horrified, Jess realized what she'd let slip. "Nothing. Forget it."

"No way. Tell me what happened, Jessie. Sit down." Cass pushed her sister toward the bed. She sat down close to her.

"Talk." The steely tone in Cass's voice could not be denied.

"It happened in fourth grade. I stayed behind to get my book bag. Mrs. Grant was standing by the door, talking to another teacher. I guess she'd forgotten about me. I heard her tell the other teacher that . . ." Jessie stopped and gulped.

"Jess, I want to hear every single word."

Jessie continued, tears in her eyes. "She couldn't believe that you and I were sisters. You were so pretty. She said that you were one of the prettiest black girls she had ever taught. Mrs. Grant talked about your pretty light skin and long straight hair. Then she told the teacher that I was just the opposite, dark skinned and funny looking." Jessie started to cry. "And that I wasn't like you at all. She told Mrs. Carson that I wasn't as smart as you or as polite . . ."

"Don't stop. Tell me all of it." Cass's voice was grim and flat.

"I don't want to!"

"Jess, you have to."

"Mrs. Grant said that I was definitely the slower sister, dumb compared to you. So she didn't expect much from me," cried Jessie, remembering the rest of the awful conversation. "She said that having me as a student was a terrible letdown after teaching you." Jessie bowed her head and cried.

"Oh! Jessie, I'm so sorry. So sorry!" Cass hugged her and rocked her back and forth.

"I took it out on you, Cass. I'm sorry for that," sobbed Jessie.

"All these years, you've been keeping that poison inside of you. Don't worry, I'll take care of Mrs. Grant," said Cass. "And anybody else who ever says anything bad about my baby sister."

"So will I," said Mrs. Williams, standing in the door. Mamatoo was behind her. They both came in and closed the door. Before Jessie knew it she was surrounded by hugs and clucks and kisses. Piece by piece, the old, hard wall inside of her cracked and collapsed.

"My beautiful Jessie," cried her mother. "If I'd only known. Darling. Jess, I've lived with those kind of people—some of them black—all my life. Why didn't you come to me?"

"For the same reason you never told me, daughter, until I read your diary, in junior high school." Mamatoo's eyes were bright with tears. "Jess felt ashamed, just like you."

In her heart Jessie knew her grandmother was right. She had been ashamed, and a huge part of her had believed that Mrs. Grant was right.

Dad knocked on the bedroom door. Everyone wiped at the tears on their face. Mom opened the door. "Yes, dear, I know it's time for dinner. Just give me a minute," she said.

Dad peered in. "I've got dinner on the table. I came to tell you to come and eat. What is going on in here?"

Mom sketched out what had happened to Jessie.

Jessie watched as her father's face swelled with fury. But his voice was calm when he asked, "And the rest? Cassandra, what is going on with you? No, don't look at each other. I'm a member of this family and I want to know. Now."

In a clear voice, Cassandra related her problems with Joe. She shared that she had decided to stop dating him until he was able to accept her position. If he wasn't then she would not date him again.

Mr. Williams leaned against the wall. He put his hands in his pockets.

"Jessie, I am a very fortunate man. I am surrounded by smart, beautiful women." He spoke slowly. "When I see your face I see a beauty and a spirit that dares to go after what she wants. That Grant woman has no business being a teacher. She's a fool. But this world is full of fools. You've got to learn to let their stupidity slide off your back like water. We'll help you."

He reached out his arms to her. Jessie got up and walked toward her father. Smiling, he met her halfway and held her close.

"Now, Cassandra, I've been waiting for this to happen. I guessed that this was the problem."

"What?" asked his wife.

"I couldn't be that stupid and still be married to you, now, could I?"

They laughed.

"But back to you, Cassandra. I'll talk to Joe, if you want me to. Frankly, I think it would be best. You should not have to carry this one by yourself. This is where having a father comes in handy. I won't embarrass you or disclose anything. You'll have to trust me."

Jessie watched her sister nod in agreement and join her in the circle of their father's arms. It felt good to have someone else carrying the load. Jessie smiled at her mother and grandmother. Such a terrible secret was out. Jess saw a few leaves blowing outside the bedroom window from the few remaining trees. The old secret felt like the old leaves—light and gone.

chapter

10

The rest of Crazy Week somersaulted by Jessie. As she
waited to walk on stage as Granny Wolf, Jessie focused
herself. It was hard to accept that her first leading role
was as a wolf disguised as a Chinese grandmother in an
ancient version of Little Red Riding Hood. She wondered if any of the African-American actresses she admired had ever taken roles like this.

Despite her misgivings, the applause at the end
of the reader's theater performance was gratifying.
With a second performance on Friday, the Halloween
Dance, and then Halloween on Saturday, the end of
the week stretched her life like an ever expanding
balloon.

Practice for the Winter Festival was moving along.
Hammering sets and painting them was not her idea of

stardom. But Jessie had accepted one thing: the infinitesimal part of Mary Ann, Harriet Tubman's younger sister, was better than nothing. *And I'm not a nothing girl,* Jessie resolved.

After the reader's theater performance on Friday, Jessie stopped by Evergreen Residential Manor. Something bothered her.

Weak sunlight lit the dayroom. Familiar faces greeted her. Jessie took out her notepad and made her way by each person, questioning them about what they might like the girls to do. The suggestions were good. By the time Jessie got to Mrs. Lee, the itch had turned into a full-blown attack. But what was bothering her?

"What a pleasant surprise! You're Jessie. Did you notice that cloudy day outside?" said Mrs. Lee. "I have memories of days like this when I lived with my son. With the gas fireplace and a good book, the gloomy afternoons seldom depressed me."

Jessie sat and listened. She heard loneliness and a tinge of regret in the older woman's voice. Her eyes sought the windows, not Jessie's face.

"People call it a fire, but it wasn't a fire. It was a firestorm. A nightmare that ruined the lives of thousands of people. Over three thousand homes and apartments burned to the ground. I still see that day in my dreams." Mrs. Lee's voice had fallen to a shaky whisper.

Jessie nodded.

"My son wants me to move back. His home is lovely.

But every time he takes me back up there, I get frightened," she said. "Even with those three crazy animals of his, especially that silly cat. I never saw a cat run sideways in my life. And such a sad cat."

Jessie's mind wandered. *There's the Halloween party. I feel hot. If I'm coming down with a cold, I won't have to go. Should I call Jamar and tell him? I need to study for the math/science test next week—*

What! A cat that runs sideways . . . What did Mrs. Lee say?

"So I just told him that I needed more time before I could make a final decision. He's my only child." Mrs. Lee smiled.

Suddenly, the itch that bothered Jessie got scratched.

"Mrs. Lee, did you say that your son has a cat that runs sideways?"

"Yes, I did. Strange, isn't it?"

"Is the cat gray? Is it a male? Does he have a half-moon scar on one leg? Is he kind of small with white feet?" The questions spilled out of Jessie's mouth like fizz out of a can of soda pop.

Mrs. Lee thought. Suddenly, she clapped her hands together.

"Jessie, do you think what I'm thinking? Could it be possible?" Her eyes shone like new pennies, then dimmed. "I can't believe I didn't make this connection sooner! Oh! This medication I have to take makes me a bit slow."

"Don't feel bad. The important thing is that we may just have a miracle here! Now, how many *yes* answers do you have to those questions?" pressed Jessie, standing up in her excitement.

"I count four—all of them! Do you have a copy of that flyer? Look over there at the table where I was playing Scrabble earlier this afternoon. I left it there with my glasses. Now why didn't I examine that photograph more closely?"

But Jessie wasn't listening. She had run to the table. Mrs. Lee reached for the flyer and the glasses. With careful deliberation her eyes moved back and forth between the photo and the written description.

"This is certainly a thorough description and a good flyer. Why didn't I pay closer attention?"

"Cooper, I mean Mkiwa, designed it. Well . . ."

"That cat is 14 Karat, I am sure of it."

"What does that name mean?"

"Oh, my son named the cat 14 Karat because he said that this cat was worth his weight in gold for being so brave. When Roy found him, he was singed from the fire and his paws were burned, but he's in good shape now," she explained.

"How can we make sure? Will your son give him back to Julie if it really is her Toby?" asked Jessie, pacing back and forth.

"Of course he will. But he's not home from work yet. In fact, he won't be back until Sunday night. He's away on business this weekend," said Mrs. Lee.

"Oh, no! We can't tell Julie yet. If we're wrong, she'd be too disappointed. We have to wait until Monday. How can we?"

Mrs. Lee looked stern. "We have no choice. Julie is too vulnerable to withstand another major disappointment. We can't tell anyone, not even the other girls in your group. I promise you that I'll phone my son as soon as I think he's home. Then I'll contact you."

Quickly, Jessie scribbled down her telephone number. "Here's my phone number. Call any time! Day or night! Please!"

It took every single iota of will that Jessie possessed not to rush to the telephone when she got home and call everyone in the group. The house was empty. After she changed clothes, Jessie started to make a sandwich. Her throat felt worse, and even though she wasn't wearing a sweater she felt hot, then cold. So she reached for a package of instant soup and made a cup.

The view from the deck spelled the coming of winter. There was an edge to the wind that meant that the trick-or-treaters would be blown from one part of the narrow, winding hill roads to another. Clouds gathered overhead, promising rain. But for some reason, she didn't mind fall leaving so winter could have its moment. Jessie knew it was largely because the terrible secret was finally out. Out in this chilly wind, blowing around. Jessie sipped the warm chicken vegetable soup. It tasted good. She went inside.

Mamatoo hurried in, rubbing her hands together.

"It's as cold as a—Whoops, I don't need to finish that sentence." She laughed. "Only four more weeks of rehearsals and we open. Jessie, you need to think long and hard about wanting to become a stage actress. This is a tough life."

Jessie coughed. "I know. I got more applause as Granny Wolf in *Lon Po Po* than I ever got in any part. Me as a wolf trying to act like a Chinese grandmother. And I was good, but, shoot, Mamatoo, this isn't exactly my dream coming true."

"Life never is. I'm proud of you, Jess. Each part is a good part. Don't ever forget that," said Mamatoo, pouring herself a cup of hot tea. "You don't sound so good. Is that cold coming back? I bet you were racing around today. Anything exciting happening?"

Jessie's insides clenched. A secret was a secret. *I wonder when these secrets will stop falling into my lap? It's tough keeping them.*

"Jessie, are you listening to me?"

Her head jerked up. It ached. "No, nothing happened. Just the same old stuff. I think I'm too sick to go to the Halloween dance. Plus I need to bring up my grade in my math/science core. The thought of getting dressed up as Sojourner Truth is too much."

"Then take your sorry self to bed, Jess. One thing. About what happened with that Mrs. Grant, how are you feeling, my beauty?" Mamatoo smiled warmly.

Jessie smiled inside. "It's funny, Mamatoo. But since I told the secret about what she said, I feel different. I didn't know . . ." She paused, her eyes suddenly tearing.

The tick-ticking of the round, red, plastic kitchen clock sounded like a *boom boom*. The feelings that Jessie believed had gone erupted. She started crying, hard crying that made her throat hurt. Mamatoo moved close.

"Just spit it out, child. These are some of the most important words you'll ever hear yourself say," she said.

Jessie swallowed. "I didn't know that Mom, Dad, and Cass loved me so much. I knew you did. But not them. Please don't tell them. It would hurt their feelings."

"Too late for that. If we learned anything, it's that if you'd been more sure of that, you wouldn't have carried that terrible secret in your heart for so long." Mamatoo sighed.

The front door burst open. The telephone rang. Praying that it was Mrs. Lee, Jessie leaped up and got it before the second ring. Mom and Cass came in together with Dad behind them. It was Joe. When Jessie told Cass, she took the phone, said about two sentences, and hung up.

"Honey, make a fire. Jessie, we need to talk with you," said her mother, hanging up coats and gesturing toward the living room.

Bewildered, Jessie sat on the couch. Mamatoo sat in an easy chair near the fireplace. Cass moved close to her sister.

"We called your old school and made an appointment earlier this week. We wanted to see Mrs. Grant,
first, without you there," said her father. "And I
wanted to talk with her principal."

"What? You mean what she said was that bad?" said
Jessie.

Mr. Williams spoke. "It was worse than bad. As far as
I am concerned her behavior was unprofessional to say
the least. She hurt you, Jessie, so much that it affected
not only your academic performance, but your self-esteem. That's very serious."

Cass walked over to Jessie. She took her hand.
"When I told Mom that I was going back to the old
school to see if she was still teaching there, Mom told
me to wait. But I didn't. I found out and wrote down
her room number."

"Thank heavens you left it in the bathroom by your
make-up." said Mrs. Williams. "That was when your
dad and I decided that we needed to get this sorted
out."

"So we met with Mrs. Grant and the principal this
afternoon," said Mr. Williams, his face serious. "For
any teacher to talk about a child that way should be il-
legal. Unfortunately, without confirmation from the
other teacher, we don't have much of a legal case. The
other teacher moved out of state. But we raised enough
of a concern that you will be receiving a personal apology from Mrs. Grant."

"I am angry. She had the gall to state that you
weren't telling the truth, that you had exaggerated

what she meant and distorted it. Those were the words she used," yelled Cass. "And all these years I thought she was such a wonderful teacher!"

Jessie sat there, blown away. All three of them had taken on Mrs. Grant for her. That teacher was going to write her an apology? Or call her? Her family had really gone to bat for her!

"You all did this for me? Why didn't you let me come?" she asked.

"Frankly, because we were afraid to, Jess. We didn't want you to be hurt more. If you want to talk to her, you can. We'll go with you. That's one option that your dad made sure the principal agreed to," said her mother.

"Mamatoo?" asked Jessie, searching for counsel.

Her grandmother smiled. "There's nothing that warms this old heart of mine more than seeing my family act the way a real family should. Living up here high on the hog can make you forget what really matters. Jess, what do you need to do?"

Cass held her hand. Jess gazed at her sister. She knew exactly what she needed.

"I need time to think. Can we talk later?"

"Yes. But we'll do it as a family," said her mother.

Dad smiled. "And that includes me."

"Jess, head downstairs and get into bed. I'll bring you something to stop that cold before it gets a hold on you," said her mother.

Relieved, Jessie got up. "I don't feel that good, but I want to go to the Halloween dance."

Her mother laughed. "This is a change! You want to go to the dance! Then we'll have to get you well."

"Thanks, Mom. And no more orange juice for me!"

They laughed.

But within hours, Jessie was running a fever. Her hopes sank. There was no way she'd be able to go to the Halloween dance. The telephone rang.

"Jess, telephone for you! And it's not a girl," yelled Cass. "Pick up the phone in our room."

Shocked, Jessie lifted the receiver. "Hi, this is Jessie Williams."

"I hope so. If it was anybody else. I'd be in trouble. This is Jamar Lewis," laughed Jamar. "Are you going to the dance?"

"I can't, Jamar. I got a cold and fever, so I have to stay in bed. I wanted to go," she said.

"Can you have company?" he asked.

Jessie didn't know what to say. "I don't know. I mean I never asked. I'll have to check with my father. OK?"

"OK. I'm on the serving committee again, so I have to go to the dance. Stay warm and get well. Bye, Jess."

"Thanks for calling, Jamar. Bye."

No matter what, Jessie stayed as close as she could to the telephone. Jamar called her over the weekend to see how she was. She hadn't garnered the nerve to ask Dad and Mom about having company. That could wait. Dealing with Cass's teasing was hard enough. Doing her math/science work in bed, propped up by sweet-smelling pillows, with cups of hot soup, and hugs was fun. By Sunday night, Mrs. Lee still hadn't called.

Late Sunday night, when she called Evergreen Residential Manor, Mrs. Lee told her that her son's flight had been delayed. She wouldn't know anything until Monday. Jessie sat on her bed and watched her sister. There was something she had to know.

"Cass, does it get easier?"

"What, Jess?"

It was difficult to figure out how to say what she wanted to. Somehow meeting with Mrs. Grant didn't make much sense. The fact that the family had stood up for her mattered much more than seeing that woman's face. But there was a larger problem.

"I don't know how to say this, Cass. But you once told me that nobody sees the real you because you're light-skinned, with straight hair and all the rest." Jessie struggled to find words.

Cass put the hair rollers aside. "You do now, at least more than you ever did."

"But not everybody?"

Cass laughed, a rueful laugh. "No and I don't think that will ever happen. But I'm standing up for myself more and not letting anybody stick me in the box they think I fit in."

Jessie thought about that. "So, it never ends. I mean, there will always be 'Mrs. Grants' around who—"

"Who have bought into those sick, ignorant ideas about what is 'beautiful.' But I'll be there for you, Jess."

"Thanks, Cass. I have to learn how to be there for myself, too. Like you are."

Cass came over and hugged her. "Then we can learn together because it sure isn't easy to do it alone."

"I know that now. Then I'm going to tell Dad and Mom that I want to see Mrs. Grant. I want her to see me and I want to see her—face to face. I don't want to ever think that part of me was too scared to see her. Will you come with me?"

"Yes. Sometimes you act like the oldest sister!" Cass shook her head.

Family Hour Monday was torture for Jess. Not saying anything about her secret made it impossible for her to do more than reply in one-word mumbles. The cold helped. It gave her an excuse.

"What's wrong with you?" Mkiwa asked.

"Yeah, Jessie."

The three girls stared at her. Only a few months ago they had been strangers. They weren't exactly family yet, but like Mr. Reynolds said, building a family took time and work. But they were learning how to become friends. What would they think when they found out that she had kept this secret from them? But if it turned out that 14 Karat wasn't Toby, then Julie would be spared a huge disappointment.

"Just tired."

"Did you get the information about what they want us to perform for them?" asked Julie.

"We need to plan and plan fast. We're due there next Monday," added Maria.

Mkiwa frowned. "We're doing much more than the other groups. Why can't we space it out more? Every other week is too often. Why not every three weeks or once a month? I've got more homework than I can finish, dance classes, and I am determined to make it to the second line, no matter what I have to do!"

"But we promised them, Cooper," Julie said.

Maria thought. "We don't all have to go each time. We could go in pairs sometimes. I'm feeling the pressure, too. But we do have to stick to the plan for next week."

"That would work. Here are the suggestions. They want to hear certain songs. Cooper, you can dance anything you want to. They just like to watch you dance. And there are some poems they want me to perform. So, Maria's idea will work." Jessie took out her notepad and shared what she had learned.

"So do we meet at your house, Maria?" asked Mkiwa.

Maria squirmed. "My father isn't feeling too well. Mama wants the house quiet, so it would be better if we met somewhere else."

Jessie spoke up. "Cooper, we never met at your house. What about Wednesday after practices?"

"No, that won't work! I mean, I have to go to the dentist that day," she said.

"Is tomorrow better?" asked Julie.

"No! My mother said something about doing something, I don't remember what," she stuttered.

Jessie eyed her. "Your mother? What about your father?"

"Let's not fight. If we can't meet at Mkiwa's house, we can meet at school," said Maria.

"We can meet at my house," said Julie. "It's really an apartment, about three blocks from where Maria lives. It's small, but everyone is welcome."

"Look, Julie, I don't want to sound rude but if we could meet at your house, next time we . . ." said Mkiwa, "shoot. We can meet at my house this time."

Julie frowned. "Are you sure you want to do this?"

"No, but I have to. My house tomorrow," said Addie Mae, her face tight as an African drum.

Jessie's preparation for her math/science report paid off. She got full points. That would please her father. But she struggled to pay attention in her history of drama class. Without Jamar there, it was harder to concentrate.

History just isn't my subject. The pile of African-American history books that Dad had brought home was in the same place it had been for weeks. There wasn't enough time.

The flurry of activity in the large performing arts theater proved that everyone felt the pressure of time running out. Onstage the directors were completing the blocking for the play. Jessie wasn't onstage much, so it was easy for her to remember where she was supposed to enter, stand, move, and exit. In the workroom next to the theater, students worked like bees in a hive, designing, cutting, attaching, and painting scenery. She spotted Jamar in a corner hammering and nailing. He looked up and waved her over.

"Here, I've been saving this hammer just for you," he said.

"I feel hammered. I don't need to hammer anything."

"You know, I'll be sorry when your red hair grows out. It fits your personality," he said. The other girls were flinging looks their way. Jessie knew they were wondering why such a handsome boy would like a plain girl like—

No. I have to stop thinking that way. Why shouldn't Jamar like me? I am smart and pretty and very talented, red hair and all, she thought. *Even if I don't believe it totally, I have to keep on trying to.*

"Well, Jamar, don't be surprised at anything I might do!" Jessie batted her eyes in mock flirtation.

The taken-aback expression on his face was worth the teasing. They laughed.

Instead of going home, Jessie went to Evergreen Residential Manor. Mrs. Lee wasn't there. She was at the hospital for a six-month checkup. There was no word from her that night. Jessie hesitated to call. She was beginning to feel like a nuisance.

Taking the bus to Addie Mae's apartment the next day took less than twenty minutes. But Addie Mae's nervousness was obvious. No one said much. Jessie glanced around. There were no family pictures. That was strange. After weeks of hearing Addie Mae drone on and on about her wonderful, loving, family-oriented father, Jessie had expected to see family photographs and mementos on the walls and end tables. But there was nothing.

In fact, there were no signs that a man even lived there. Jessie went into the kitchen. No photographs on the refrigerator or even schedules. Nothing. The telephone rang. Addie Mae quickly answered it. Jessie could barely hear the short string of "yes," "no," and "I'll see" answers. Whoever she was talking to wasn't someone she felt very comfortable with.

They had selected the songs they would perform by the time Mrs. Cooper came home. She looked tired. Addie Mae had taken out potato chips and soda pop. No one was very hungry.

"It's good to see your friends here. I was wondering when you'd invite them over," Mrs. Cooper said, hanging up her coat and thumbing through the mail. "How's the planning going?"

"Fine," the girls responded in unison.

"Addie, did your—" she started to ask.

"Mama, please, I have to talk to you about something! Right now."

Before Mrs. Cooper could utter another word, her daughter had grabbed her arm and pushed her into a bedroom off the hallway. The girls heard the loud slam of the bedroom door. The voices inside got louder and louder. After about ten minutes, Addie Mae came out. It was clear that she had been crying.

Jessie had handed them all their coats. Whatever

was going on in this house was none of their business. One look at Addie Mae's stricken face made Jessie regret the way she had pushed her about coming over.

"Look, don't say anything. I'm sorry I gave you a hard time. We got the work done. We'll see you tomorrow, Cooper," said Jessie, as she handed Julie her crutches.

"Thanks."

Jessie glanced back once as they walked down the stairs. Addie Mae stood in the doorway. She looked so lonely and forlorn. Sometimes Jessie liked Addie Mae, and other times, the girl got on her last nerves. But everybody had a right to her own secrets. If anyone knew that, she did.

When Jess got home, there was a message on the answering machine from Mrs. Lee. Jessie punched the numbers as fast as she could. Finally, Mrs. Lee came to the telephone.

"Jessie, I'm sorry, but life got out of hand for awhile," she said.

"Did you talk to your son? Is the cat Toby?"

"Yes, I did talk with him. He's willing to bring the cat down here tomorrow about 4:00 P.M. That's the earliest he can come, unless you can wait until the weekend."

"No! This can't wait. I'll have us there. But what if it's not Toby? What will we do?" asked Jessie.

Mrs. Lee was silent. "You told me that the most important thing, your teacher said, was for the four of you

to try. This is the best try you've had so far. We'll have
to wait and see."

Jessie called Julie, Maria, and Addie Mae as soon as
she hung up. She made up a story about Mrs. Winters
wanting to see them about their project the next day,
Wednesday, at four. Everyone bought it.

That night Jessie barely slept. Having to go through
the day keeping the secret gave her a headache. By the
time they got to Evergreen Residential Manor, she was
exhausted. Mrs. Lee was in the dayroom with other
seniors. But her son wasn't there.

"Where's Mrs. Winters?" asked Addie Mae.

"Hi, Mrs. Lee. How are you feeling?" asked Julie.

"Just fine, Julie. Nice of you to ask. Girls, pull up
some chairs," she directed. "I have something—well,
Jessie and I have something to tell you."

Just then her son walked in holding a gray cat with
white paws. Jessie froze. Julie stood absolutely still.
Her crutches fell to the floor. The other two girls
looked from one to the other.

"Toby! Toby!" cried Julie, limping toward the cat.

With a sound somewhere between anguish and joy,
the cat keened, and sprang from the man's arms. Jessie
watched him run toward Julie. He started off at an
angle, running sideways!

Julie managed to bend down and sit on the floor.
The cat leaped into her arms. He nuzzled her face and
purred as she scratched him behind his ear.

"Julie, check behind his leg," urged Jessie.

She bent down, too. The half-moon scar stood out clearly. There was no doubt in anyone's mind that this was Toby. Julie sobbed as she held her cat. It was as if she was crying for all of the bad days, weeks, and months since the firestorm. Toby licked her face. Even Addie Mae had tears in her eyes.

"Jessie, you did it? You found Toby?" asked Maria.

Jessie shook her head. "No, Mrs. Lee did. We all did. If it wasn't for Cooper's flyer and all of our work, this would have never happened."

"And a miracle," said Mrs. Lee, squeezing her son's hand.

"As much as I like 14 Karat, I mean, Toby, he belongs home. Just like your flyer said, 'Bring a fire victim home.' I never saw him act so excited about anything," he said.

"Oh, thank you, thank all of you so much," cried Julie, her eyes shining. "Thanks for getting Toby back to me."

Jessie grinned, knowing that it was possible for miracles to happen. But even miracles required enormous effort and energy.

"This deserves a song," said Maria. She went to the piano and began playing "For He's a Jolly Good Fellow."

"We'll have to come up with a different show," whispered Addie Mae. "One about Julie and Toby—a celebration show."

"That's a great idea! You don't mind meeting again?" Jessie asked.

Addie Mae looked away. "Nope. Having something special like this to celebrate feels good. I'll work on a cat dance."

"I'll get a copy of the play *Cats* and see if there is something in there I could do," added Jessie.

"Maybe Maria can perform the music. And Julie can sit in the audience and hold Toby."

Jessie clapped. "Addie Mae, you are brilliant! Oh, I'm sorry, I meant Cooper."

Addie Mae sighed. "My name thing is getting complicated, isn't it? I know. I'm going to have to figure out what to do."

Jessie knew what that felt like. "Don't rush. I'll call you whatever you want."

Addie Mae gave Jessie a long, searching look. "Thanks. But I'm tired of this. Look, my mother and father are divorced. My father married some woman a few weeks after the divorce. That was a year ago. Then she got pregnant. They just had a baby boy. I don't see my daddy much anymore. That's why I named myself Mkiwa. I feel like an orphan. So now you know. Call me Addie Mae. Changing my name didn't make me feel better."

The girls were stunned.

"We're sorry," said Jessie. "We didn't know."

Julie put her hand on Addie Mae's arm. "I know. My parents argue all the time. The fire caused so many problems. My father wants to rebuild, but my mother just wants to move somewhere else. It's horrible going home. I hope they don't get divorced."

"Addie Mae, I feel dumb," said Maria. "I'm sorry."

Addie Mae managed a wan smile. "I thought that if I told you, you all would . . . I was scared that you would think less of me."

"Looks like Jessie is the only one who doesn't have something bothering her. You're lucky, Jessie," said Maria.

Jessie looked at the Fours, Maria, Addie Mae, and Julie with Toby in her arms. She remembered that first day in school. They had been so different and separate. Not anymore. They had learned so much about one another—Maria's worries about her father's angina, Julie and the devastation of the fire, and Addie Mae's split family. *But nothing about me. Nothing that really counts. If Addie Mae could speak out, I have to.*

"No, I'm not lucky, Maria. There's something you should know. Something that happened to me in fourth grade. It's had a lot to do with the way I've acted, especially toward you, Addie Mae," said Jessie, her palms sweaty.

The girls moved closer together as Jessie related what Mrs. Grant had said and what had happened. When she finished, she kept her head down. *I don't want to see pity in their eyes.* Finally, she lifted her head. She didn't see pity, just caring and tears.

"Oh, Jessie, I wish I looked like you!" said Addie Mae. "You're the beautiful one! I see that happen all the time. Grown-ups liking light-skinned African-American kids like me the best! And white—and black—people smiling at me. I keep trying to make everybody know that I am proud of being an African-American. Maybe I try too hard . . . I stay mixed up."

Jessie smiled. "The two of us are some pair."

The others chimed in. They surrounded Jessie. Toby purred in Julie's arms.

Julie handed him to Jessie. "You hold Toby. I don't understand this color stuff. I know about racism and prejudice, but I didn't know how African-Americans felt about their own differences of skin color. What I do know a lot about is feeling lost, hurt, and alone. If we stick together, the four of us can make it at OPA. No matter what happens."

Jessie grinned at Julie. Then at Addie Mae and Maria. She started their chant. "Four, three, two, one. We're the best. Let's have some fun!" With Toby in the center, they chanted and laughed.

Mrs. Williams came and got them. One by one the girls were dropped off. Jessie helped carry Toby to the door for Julie. Before she left, Julie turned and hugged Jessie.

On the way home, Jessie told her mother the entire story. After awhile she fell silent. While her mother talked about Thanksgiving plans, Jessie drifted off. Thanksgiving was three weeks away. Between now and then she had so much to do at the Oakland Performing Arts Middle School.

Thanksgiving had come early this year for the Fours. *Our first Thanksgiving and it was wonderful! Nobody's problems are solved, but at least we each made a start.*

Jessie opened her eyes. Sprinkles of rain dotted the

windshield. The wipers swept back and forth in graceful arcs. A gray sheen covered the sky. Fall was ending. The winter rains were on their way. They passed her favorite tree. It stood defiant and sturdy even as the rain and winds pounded away at it.

Jessie sighed. Fall had stripped away most of the brave red leaves. She peered closely. There were just a few still hanging on.

Warm and snug in the station wagon, Jessie felt comforted knowing that at the places where the leaves had been blown away, new growth waited. Minuscule and fragile, growing buds would couch inside of the tree branches until it was time to burst forth, green and alive.

Jessie smiled. She wanted to wave good-bye to the tree. But it would only be a temporary good-bye. That was the precious secret of fall.